The Journey Prize Anthology

Winners of the $10,000 Journey Prize

1989
Holley Rubinsky (of Toronto, Ont., and Kaslo, B.C.)
for "Rapid Transits"

1990
Cynthia Flood (of Vancouver, B.C.)
for "My Father Took a Cake to France"

1991
Yann Martel (of Montreal, Que.)
for "The Facts Behind the Helsinki Roccamatios"

1992
Rozena Maart (of Ottawa, Ont.)
for "No Rosa, No District Six"

1993
Gayla Reid (of Vancouver, B.C.)
for "Sister Doyle's Men"

1994
Melissa Hardy (of London, Ont.)
for "Long Man the River"

1995
Kathryn Woodward (of Vancouver, B.C.)
for "Of Marranos and Gilded Angels"

1996
Elyse Gasco (of Montreal, Que.)
for "Can You Wave Bye Bye, Baby?"

1997 (shared)
Gabriella Goliger (of Ottawa, Ont.)
for "Maladies of the Inner Ear"

Anne Simpson (of Antigonish, N.S.)
for "Dreaming Snow"

1998
John Brooke (of Montreal, Que.)
for "The Finer Points of Apples"

The Journey Prize Anthology

Short Fiction from the Best of
Canada's New Writers

Selected with Sheldon Currie

M&S

Canadian Cataloguing in Publication Data

The National Library of Canada has catalogued this publication as follows:

Main entry under title:

The Journey Prize anthology:
the best short fiction from Canada's literary journals

Annual.
1–
Subtitle varies.
ISSN 1197-0693
ISBN 0-7710-4424-0 (v. 11)

1. Short stories, Canadian (English).*
2. Canadian fiction (English) – 20th century.*

PS8329.J68   C813'.0108054   C93-039053-9
PR9197.32.J68

We acknowledge the financial support of the Government of Canada through the Book Publishing Industry Development Program for our publishing activities. We further acknowledge the support of the Canada Council for the Arts and the Ontario Arts Council for our publishing program. Canada

Typeset in Trump Mediaeval by M&S, Toronto

Printed and bound in Canada

McClelland & Stewart Inc.
The Canadian Publishers
481 University Avenue
Toronto, Ontario
M5G 2E9

1 2 3 4 5   03 02 01 00 99

About the Journey Prize Anthology

The $10,000 Journey Prize is awarded annually to a new and developing writer of distinction. This award, now in its eleventh year, is made possible by James A. Michener's generous donation of his Canadian royalty earnings from his novel *Journey*, published by McClelland & Stewart Inc. in 1988. The winner of this year's Journey Prize, to be selected from among the twelve stories in this book, will be announced in October 1999.

The Journey Prize Anthology comprises a selection from submissions made by literary journals across Canada, and, in recognition of the vital role journals play in discovering new writers, McClelland & Stewart makes its own award of $2,000 to the journal that has submitted the winning entry. In keeping with the national reach of the anthology, this is the second year in which the selection jury has met outside Toronto. Last year, the judging was done in Vancouver by a West Coast jury, and this year the three jurors – Sheldon Currie, author of *The Glace Bay Miners' Museum*, the novel that became the successful film *Margaret's Museum*; writer/academic/publisher Lesley Choyce; and bookseller Mary Jo Anderson of Frog Hollow Books – met in Halifax.

This year's cover illustration is by Genevieve Bismonte, and was selected from submissions made by the Ontario College of Art and Design's illustration classes.

The Journey Prize Anthology has established itself as one of the most prestigious anthologies in the country. It has become a who's who of up-and-coming writers, and many of the authors whose early work has appeared in the anthology's pages have gone on to single themselves out with collections of short stories and literary awards. The Journey Prize itself is the most significant monetary award given in Canada to a writer at the beginning of his or her career for a short story or excerpt from a fiction work in progress.

McClelland & Stewart would like to acknowledge the continuing enthusiastic support of writers, literary journal editors, and the public in the common celebration of the emergence of new voices in Canadian fiction.

Contents

MIKE BARNES

In Florida

By moonlight, the drooping bellshaped flowers
hanging from a small tree are a waxy,
                                    khaki colour.
The banana tree's large fringed leaves, broad enough to
serve as roofing or an umbrella, shelter
the bright green fruit in a cluster just beginning to
                                     separate,
like a green hand forming, not a trace of IGA yellow.
Pines, palmettos. Amaryllis.
Hibiscus in luscious, postcard red, its stamens hungry-looking.
The spiky-leaved pineapple palm, its latticework
sides peeling off as it grows leaving smooth grey bark,
the shed strips lying around the base;
out of the tufted hair like excelsior a lizard
                                crawls by starlight,
a retiree like me.

                        ~

The Atwaters landed in Fort Myers at 7 p.m. After picking up
their rental car, they drove to Punta Gorda with the windows
down, exclaiming that they could do such a thing even though
it was rather chilly. The air was moist and fragrant. Nan Atwater
wondered if it could be oranges that gave it such a sweet, faintly
citrusy perfume. Les said she was imagining that.

I

After a snack of Lipton's Cup-o'-Soup, they decided to take a walk around the compound. That was what Mrs. Fairleigh, the owner of their "unit," had called Sunset Estates when she gave them their key. "She makes it sound like a prison," Nan whispered as they left her door, Mrs. Fairleigh shooting safety bolts behind them.

"It's what they're all called," Les said.

"Or a barracks. Did you notice, her perfume smells like Lemon Pledge?"

Les pointed to some pale green fruits on staked trees about three feet high. The soil around the saplings was dark in the moonlight; it had been turned recently. Plastic name tags were affixed to the stakes. *Lemon, Date Palm.* Les read them out and they walked on. "I don't think they needed to label everything," Nan said. "It's not a museum."

Les nodded soberly. Patient and reserved by nature, he had become more so in his chosen career. For thirty years he had worked as an epidemiologist, someone who tracks the spread of disease and suggests ways of controlling it. He was trained to see trends, the big picture that might or might not lurk behind the single detail. That was why it was so alarming to him these days to find himself preoccupied with an isolated report. Front-line sightings led so easily to panic or denial. *They only had their arms around each other's waists*, he would catch himself thinking; *since when is friendship a crime? Fourteen. Fourteen's not a baby.* He was rationalizing and retrenching like an outback medic in the face of some startling symptom. But this was not Patient X, the carrier of a new or old plague. It was his son, Dennis.

∿

The next morning, Les sat on the sofa and thought about what he might write. His hour was almost over. Nan had roughed in a sky. The only thing that came to mind was that he had chosen the wrong hobby, but he had already recorded that in an earlier entry.

Find a hobby. How many times had he heard that at his retirement brunch? Nan had got the same thing at the gallery shop where she had worked part-time. As if they were being advised to compose a last message to posterity. A parting shot. Nan began to paint pictures, watercolours, always of a lake or river, with a tree on the shore, and then, when she improved a bit, sometimes with a bird on the branch of the tree. Birds were hard. Meant to be delicate, flight-capable, they tended to come out as lumps, clods stuck to the scene instead of alighting on it. After flirting with woodcarving, gardening, and French cooking, Les decided to keep a journal. "Not a diary," he told Nan. "Who wants to know what I had for breakfast?" Each morning, for exactly an hour, he recorded his observations. He made some discoveries about writing. A description – of anything – started to sound like a poem if you broke up the line lengths. There were many things you could think but not write, since writing was a kind of doing. He tried not to censor himself, though he assumed he was.

"Finished scratching?" Nan called, and Les, smiling, closed his book. Her own hobby was *doodling*.

After lunch they took another walk. The sun felt clean, unreal, more Lemon Pledge. The compound was surrounded with high brick walls. Beyond the walls was Florida, its malls and swamps, too dangerous to explore except from a car. A woman with platinum hair and mahogany skin, wearing tight green shorts and a cerise singlet, nodded as she speedwalked by. Nan's raised eyebrow promised a name. Jiggles, maybe. Or Silicon.

Where the asphalt forked at a clump of palm trees, one side becoming a dirt lane that led, judging from the fishy smell, down to the docks, the Atwaters were startled by a large grey turtle that emerged from the bushes and began crossing the roadway towards the seaward side. Its forelegs were like flippers, swimming across the asphalt; its rear legs were bowed and clomping, unclawed.

They stood for a few moments, watching it.

Les took a step, and the turtle retracted its head and stopped. When he touched the back of its shell with his toe, the head shot out, twisting back with a hiss. Les stumbled back with the look of comical shock that delighted Nan as much, and as often, as her names did him; not just his exaggerated fright, but his surprise at it.

After they had resumed walking, she remarked that the turtle's shell looked like a German army helmet. Les saw it instantly, wondering why he hadn't seen it first. There was a time when he had fallen asleep every night seeing those helmets, plus tanks, machine guns, all of it. He had been eight in 1939.

"Fore!" a man called, as a golf ball rose up from behind a bush and plonked onto the next lawn. Another ball lay near it on the grass, nestled like two white eggs. Two thin, tanned men in pastel outfits appeared, each carrying a single iron. They would be the chippers Mrs. Fairleigh had complained about, her voice rising with the fear of broken windows. One man touched his cap at Nan. Their cleats clattered briefly on the pavement.

∾

Two days after the Atwaters arrived, there was a reception for them and other newcomers. It was organized by the social committee and held in the lounge beside the pool. Scoping out the room earlier, Nan had seen bright blue broadloom stretching not quite to the beige walls, showing a border of bare concrete. A vacuum cleaner stood in the middle of the room, its cord running to the wall. Nan imagined a black woman eating her lunch somewhere. A bookcase with paperbacks had the look of being stocked by forgetful guests. Nan felt the emptiness of the room, like space she could touch. She shut the door and hurried out to the pool with its tennis ball sun lobbed into blue, a frail old lady wading.

Now, however, the rec room was lively with conversation, two card tables jaunty with bowls of chips and peanuts. It was BYOB, but ice in plastic bowls and a generous selection of mixers had been provided.

The Atwaters joined a group near the mixer table that included another Canadian couple, the Garries, a stringy pair from Indiana called the Brittels, and a tall handsome man with thick grey hair and a sullen expression who was introduced by John Brittel as Senator Stone, from Wisconsin.

"I wish you wouldn't keep saying that," said the senator. "You know I lost the election."

John Brittel shrugged, smiling. "What can you do?" He

addressed the four Canadians. "It was the Democrats' year. Give Clinton two years to screw things up and then he'll be in again."

This observation seemed to increase Mr. Stone's sourness. He left to refill his glass, and Helen Brittel clamped a hand on Nan's arm. "He's dying. Cancer," she muttered, then smiled at the returning Mr. Stone.

Nan, not knowing what to say, caught Sue Garrie's glance. She seemed to peep out from the shade of her large, quiet husband, Oscar. "Wish we had anyone even half as good," Sue said, adding vaguely, "as any of them."

The four Canadians nodded at each other but did not enlarge on the political situation back home. No one had asked them to. The three Americans were looking around the room.

"More fresh meat," John Brittel shot an elbow at Les's side and gestured with his glass at the door, where another pale couple had entered and were in the process of being absorbed by a tanned group.

"Yes. I see," said Les. Something in Brittel attracted him, some shrewdness, not without its cruelty, that was partly hidden by a jocular manner. At least, thought Les, he seemed to be making an effort to size up situations, to analyze them. His brain was working.

"Watch yourself in the sun at first," Helen said to Nan, her talon-like ringers on her arm again. "You'll see the locals in sweaters, they think it's cold. But don't be fooled."

Nan nodded, grateful in the same way Les had been for the other's woman's snaring certainty. Across the circle, which seemed already to have subdivided, she could see Sue Garrie trying to draw out the dying former senator on his political career, Oscar smiling and nodding above them.

They walked back from the party with the Brittels, whose unit was near theirs. The apartments were boxy but attractive, with white stucco walls and red tile roofs – "Spanish," as Mrs. Fairleigh had promised. Unfortunately, yellow tape, like a police line, had had to be strung up on poles beyond the borders of flowering shrubs, after a botanically minded tenant had been nearly brained by a falling tile.

John Brittel walked with a cane they had not noticed during the social; it had leaned against the wall behind him and he had snatched it deftly when it was time to go. Why he needed it was unclear. He felt free to gesture with it, and moved it ahead with a little circling flourish in the air.

The Brittels declined the Atwaters' offer of a nightcap with wide eyes and windy renunciations.

"Don't tempt us!" Helen said.

"You settle in!" John ordered. "You get a couple of old souses like us in the door and you'll never get to bed."

Smiles went round the group. The Brittels said goodnight. They had only gone a few steps away when John hurried back, leading with the cane.

"How do you feel about fishing?" he asked Les.

Les said that he had done some, years ago.

"Check the local news tomorrow morning," John advised. "Bunch of us go down on the pier after sea trout. Come on down with us! You get 'em when the tide's coming in or out. Half-hour before's when we start. Good night!"

He was on his way back when Helen Brittel skittered over to Nan. Nan smelled her stale breath and felt the imploring strong fingers; but Helen's eyes were warm under the streetlight.

"You a fisherwoman?"

Nan shook her head.

"Good! We'll get our beauty tan and have a little gab while the men catch dinner!" She started back. John was leaning on his cane, waiting. "At the pool!" she called.

Les poured them each a rye and sat down on the couch with Nan. "The Stayners again?" he asked, sipping. Nan smiled and shook her head: no way! This was an old joke, their tendency to pick up strays. It had begun on their honeymoon, forty years before, when a white-haired couple named the Stayners had monopolized their time. "Do we look lonely?" Nan asked. Les shrugged; this too was an old question. They watched the eleven o'clock news, most of the half-hour taken up with crime. There was a murder and rape in Tampa, along with several local beatings and robberies. The national news shrank to make room for it.

Lizard sentry,
2-3" long, mottled grey-brown, pops up
*   suddenly on the screen,*
standing erect and vigilant, head and one leg raised
* like a pointer dog,*
tolerating approach within a certain range,
darting away when an invisible line is crossed.

Sipping coffee, preening full light.
Hope he comes back
Waiting to tell Nan, still on the phone to Dennis.

Dennis is fine, sends love. No sign of him.
Continuing then: last night's scream, probably a bobcat;
the egrets gracefully stalking the mud flats at low tide,
* fine white strands lifted*
from the backs of their heads by the slightest breeze;

the pelican that landed on top of the condo complex
and made a series of interesting, quite peculiar silhouettes,
as he shifted in various positions.

∾

In the night Les woke to the sound of Nan crying. Opening his eyes, he saw light leaking around the top and bottom of the bathroom door. It was where she usually went. She would be sitting on the toilet, a Kleenex held under her nose and others bunched in the hand resting, palm up, in her lap. He had only opened the door once, but the picture had branded him, its details seared across some tough hide in his consciousness.

He raised himself to a sitting position and put the pillow behind him. He switched on the bedside lamp and opened his Le Carré novel. The words swam and blurred; he was too tired to read. He stared at the lighted rectangle; when he heard the water run he narrowed his gaze. It was what she wanted from him. Not a hug, not comforting words, but the knowledge that he was similarly afflicted. That whatever was keeping her up had attacked him too. He listened. Her sniffling was faint and steady. Dennis.

Later, after they had both been reading for an hour or so, Les put down his book. He looked around the new bedroom, blinking. Concentrating on the story had not only brought him fully awake, but the print had become so vividly real that it had dislodged his surroundings. The letters were like little black rivets holding down a brilliant fluttering picture so he could see it. Now he turned from the picture to the shadowy room, as a painter might turn from an absorbing canvas to a studio in which dusk has fallen, and saw shadowy, ordinary things, slowly becoming familiar. A print of ibises. Floral-patterned curtains, vaguely vegetative swirls. The cushioned wicker chair and glass-topped wicker table Mrs. Fairleigh was so proud of.

Here. In Florida, he reminded himself. Punta Gorda. Winter. Retirement.

Reaching for the lamp, he said, "We better see about getting some sleep. John and Helen look like crack-of-dawners to me."

"Hm. I'll bet," Nan said, with her bracing hint of acid.

In the dark, Les found her hand under the covers. He had said the right thing at the right time. Marriage, he sometimes thought, the core of it, was the development of a language peculiar to two people, a grammar, a syntax, a rhythm, a vocabulary. Sometimes, communicating a great deal with a look or touch, or with silence, one could feel eloquent.

They lay in the dark a while like that, not speaking. Les's hand over Nan's, before falling asleep.

～

Dennis was their second son. Four months ago, he had been accused of pedophilia. No charges had been laid; only one incident, relatively minor, was known to have occurred, and the parents of the boy he had embraced at the chess club felt that further damage to their son could be avoided by "low-balling" the incident. Les, struggling to meet Vic Brittmuir's eyes during their awkward coffee together, had to look away at this phrase.

It made Dennis sound like a poor investment, a wrong turn – thoughts Les had had himself about his "different" – "arty," Nan said – youngest child. David, performing well at expected intervals, was the family's blue-chip stock.

Dennis was to seek counselling, for his alcohol problem as well as his sexual inclinations; this was the gist of the informal agreement that was reached in the Brittmuirs' den, Mrs. Brittmuir, barred from the discussion of male aberrations, silently refilling coffee cups and then backing out of sight, like a butler in drag. "Civilized," Nan remarked, when Les returned home and told her. She continued cutting her potatoes into precise lengths, with a *thunk, thunk, thunk* on the cutting board that sounded like a fist upon a door.

Purely in terms of providing a focus during a blank spot, Dennis's trouble came at the right time. It came when Les was first beginning to feel the real strain of filling his days. Summer, though he knew he was retired, had felt much as usual. Then September and October had been busy, and had felt productive, as they planned their winter south. They did this conscientiously, comparing rates and climates, debating the relative virtues of Florida and Arizona and coastal Texas, finally settling on Mrs. Fairleigh and her "lovely property." That was when Nan began to notice the change in Les that she had been waiting for. It crept into his solid competence – a hint of vacancy, a befuddled air that offended her somewhat. Les had never been befuddled. Confused, yes, but that made him annoyed, not fussy and maundering like a forgetful housekeeper, taking much of the morning to follow a bran muffin recipe. He had even begun, quite suddenly, to walk like an old man, stooping a little and taking mincing steps.

Dennis's crisis seemed to jolt him back to himself. The evidence that he was still needed as a father in the original sense, as an adult responsible for a child, seemed to bolster him. It was his idea to invite Dennis to stay at home while they were gone, though he accentuated the "house-sitting" aspect of the arrangement a little too heavily, Nan felt. Dennis was twenty-six. Their "afterthought" – ten years after David – but hardly a kid. But

Dennis agreed to stay, and sat quietly while Les went over the "house rules," which Nan had to leave the room for.

~

Once, Les had visited the chess club, soon after Dennis had been elected president. Les had taught the game to his sons, but had not played himself in years. He went mainly in order to see Dennis succeeding at something. They met at Mother's and had a pizza together, after Dennis had closed Planets, the sci-fi used bookstore owned by his longtime friend, Martin. They walked up the street to the YWCA, and Les watched, pleased, as Dennis unlocked a games cupboard and directed several boys in setting up the boards and clocks and informed them about an upcoming ladder tournament. Other club members arrived and Les played a series of speed chess games with an old man from Eastern Europe who always lost on time but refused to set the clocks to a more generous interval. Near the end of the night, Les took pleasure in being checkmated by his son, to the delight of a circle of onlookers. It was painful now to search his memory of those grinning young faces for another reason. Thinking: That one? Or him? Him?

~

In the days that followed, Les and Nan noted the same linkings of tanned and pale faces they had seen in the rec room: swimming, taking walks, playing the chipping game, shopping at the mall. As it can at a dance, the accident of first-met seemed to lay down a law, a claim. Every group had its leaders, like the Brittels, and its followers, like themselves. And each group had a couple that Nan thought of as "in reserve," like the Garries, people not unattractive, but not sought out. Even loners, like Mr. Stone and his seldom-seen wife, orbited a particular group like moons.

News was exchanged, around the pool or on the dock, according to certain rules. Questions on both career and children were expected – to leave either out would seem odd – but they were handled differently. Detailed questions on one's former job, or "line" as John Brittel put it, were welcome. Viewed under an earned sun, a job seemed a thing apart from oneself; one could rue it like rain.

Sometimes, a former career offered a clue to a personality. Late in the afternoon, when the Garries had ended their shuffleboard playing and Sue had gone for a quick dip, splashing in the shallow end while exclaiming how refreshing it was (the other women watched her closely the first time but then not again), Oscar Garrie, wearing a faded brown outfit that looked as if it had been worn on many vacations, many walks along the beach, wandered over to the pier where the men were fishing to see what had been caught. He ambled along the weathered planks, pausing to look in the plastic pails used for bait and caught fish. Asking the name of a fish he hadn't seen before, and was it good to eat?

He stopped and stood behind Les and John. After a few moments, he said in a thick, slow voice, "Watcha' usin' for bait?"

Les, always quick to include an outsider, set his pole down with a clunk and opened the lid of the shrimp bucket he and John were sharing. John had driven up to the bait shop in his Cadillac that morning. The shrimp were mostly dead already, pink-grey and strong-smelling.

"Shrimp, eh?" The large man squatted to see them better and Les was aware of a clean soapy odour coming from his close-shaved face, ruddy and large-pored. He saw his small, intelligent eyes taking in the shrimp with interest, fastening on them.

When Oscar had moved on, John said, "He used to be a judge," delivering the comment straight out at Charlotte Harbour.

"*Did he*?" Les said. It made sense. The slowness, the apart-ness, the settled habits. He saw the present Oscar sitting in his comfortable chinos, behind a raised bench in an empty court-room, his judgment suspended until it was needed again.

At the end of the pier, Oscar stood for a few minutes with his hands in his pockets, rocking back and forth. He put his hand up to see something against the sun. Cars crawled over the distant bridge; boats passed under it. Gulls wheeled and pelicans flapped up and dove down. He made a dark silhouette. After a while he passed behind them on his way back, his footsteps soft for a big man. Les saw him walk past John's Cadillac at the foot of the pier, his hands in his pockets, and disappear.

"A judge, eh?" said Don Rickert, a Pennsylvanian fishing on the other side of John. "I imagine he's seen a few things, all right." There was respect, perhaps pity, in his voice.

That, too, was apt: seen some things. An excuse, a condition and a privilege: it was all of these.

Children were another matter. Questions about them should be kept breezy, at first anyway. Children were not past in the way jobs were. Or, the happiest, simplest years were past, and the dangerous years were at hand. They were the likely occasion of griefs: divorce, mental problems, worsening habits.

It was Helen Brittel, on the Atwaters' second visit to the pool, who, in her bright, brassy voice, brought up the question Les and Nan feared and had not discussed.

"So, who's holding the Atwater fort back in Canada?"

The Atwaters could not look at each other.

"Well –" Les began, and Nan jumped in.

"Two sons. Dennis runs a bookstore; he's minding the house right now. Mother's a little paranoid, don't you know. Our oldest boy, David, is an architect. Nancy and he live in Peterborough. Jacob, their first, came along about a year ago."

Helen lifted her dark glasses slowly up her forehead and looked straight at them. Her arm was lifted as if to summon the attention of the other loungers. Les felt his stomach region go cold.

"Chips off the old block," she said, incredibly.

Les could not look at Nan. Then, suddenly, he took in the meaning of Helen's uplifted arm. It was a gesture at the table between him and Nan, on which lay Nan's sketchbook and his own paperback. Instantly, his fear of Helen and resentment of her probing turned to admiration for her quickness, a respect that was close to awe. Sketching and writing: architecture and bookselling – why had his mind never drawn a line between these activities?

Energized by their relief, Les and Nan went for a dip. "Race you," Nan called, and was halfway down the pool before Les could mobilize himself. He almost caught up to her on the return, smacking the end of the pool with his leading arm and standing, winded, to hear the laughter and the cheers. John Brittel was squatting just above him, holding Nan's arm aloft. Blinking chlorinated water from his eyes, Les saw Nan smiling at him, heard the applause. Only former senator Stone was stiff facing the other way, ignoring someone else's win.

Shrimp as bait, as food, turning pink-grey as they die.

The "love bugs," flying in pairs joined at the abdomen; proceeding slowly and erratically, pulling in opposite directions.

(Nan is taking one of her "wrist-savers," as she calls her breaks from her watercolours. Looking out the window towards the marsh, her hands on her lap. One advantage of my kind of painting: no one can tell you're not working, since thinking is half of it. I wish one of the lizards would pop up for her. Both our hobbies are coming along. She says her pictures don't look like anything. I tell her neither do mine – yet! Notes is a better word than poems, I think. Less pretentious. One possibly hopeful sign is that Helen says I look like the "studious type." So Nan says anyway. John just talks about money, his arthritis, and what bait works best. Good company, though.

❧

Mr. Stone was an odd duck. Nobody liked him much. That was why he was still called the senator, sometimes even to his face. By now this brought only a frown and a tired wave. He seemed vain, and his illness, which in another would have inspired sympathy, seemed part of his vanity. There was an ostentation to his stiff, wounded walk, the precise hours he spent in the sun, not reading, not talking, turning every few minutes, as if dedicated solely to absorbing whatever helpful energy the sun could offer him. His marriage was assumed to be bad, since his younger wife seldom accompanied him to the pool, preferring to shop with friends. She had been his secretary and had married him for his money; uncertain about his will, she was going to enjoy it now – the rumours began to arrange themselves in sequence.

One day, Nan ran into him in Publix. Les was next door at Eckerd's, checking the specials on pop and beer. Mr. Stone nodded dolefully at her as she pushed her cart past his. There was something about him that Nan liked: his formality was like the portico to a mansion where one could stop and talk awhile, sheltered between the lawn and the door, close to both; though after noticing this attraction – really no more than the space where an attraction could exist – she had not thought about it further.

After filling her cart, she ran into him again. He was standing with a package of bacon in his hand, looking over it at other packages. Nan recalled that his wife's name was Zeeta. Tall and slim, he bent forward stiffly, the bacon slices near his chest. There was a solemnity, and an absurdity, about him. A natural gravity coexisting with a natural lightness – it confused Nan.

Dying alone, she thought, then frowned. No, that wasn't it. Strange, she thought, how the dream keeps springing up with the oddest people: the dream of bypassing all the usual channels and ways and means of getting to know someone, of attaining limited knowledge of them, in order to find someone whom one knows at a glance, all through. No more steps, ploys, gambles, hard work: just communion. It was something like that, strangely enough, that she sensed was possible between Mr. Stone and herself. Not romance, necessarily, though the dream could take that form: the dream of truly knowing someone. It frightened Nan.

Les was putting his stash of American beers in the trunk when she came out. Excitedly, they compared the deals they had found, exaggerating their pleasure unthinkingly. Bargain-hunting seemed an important part of retirement, a prowess that could actually grow with advancing years.

～

One raw day most of the regulars stayed away from the pool. Nan found herself alone with Mr. Stone. He was lying on a chaise longue with a towel under his head and his eyes closed. He had on a short terrycloth jacket; goosebumps stippled his bare legs. Nan sat down at a table under an umbrella and opened her *Vanity Fair*, concentrating hard on an article about a dead model in order to block out the breeze. After a while she opened her sketchbook, thinking that a little activity might warm her up.

At a sound behind her, she turned. Mr. Stone had swung his long legs over the side of the chaise and was sitting up, facing her.

"Homesick?" he said. After a moment Nan thought he might be referring to the coolness and the grey, scudding clouds.

"Oh, gosh no," she said. She went on quickly. "This is nothing. Back home, they'd give their eye teeth for a day like this." She stopped, suddenly uncertain.

Mr. Stone was nodding slowly. It was strange, the way he was looking at her: just looking, as he might look at anything that interested him. Nan became embarrassed. *He hasn't got long*, she found herself thinking; and at the thought his face became decipherable. He was lonely.

"We've been talking for two minutes and you haven't asked me about my political career," he said with a faint, wry smile.

"I'm sure you've heard enough about that."

"And you have, too."

Nan laughed nervously. "We do go on here, don't we?"

Mr. Stone reached up and rubbed the back of his neck. The cloth jacket parted to show more of his slim brown chest with its long silver hairs. "Or my health?"

Nan blushed. "That's your business. I *am* sorry you're not feeling well." Mr. Stone nodded slowly again. Looking up at the sky, he asked, "Canadian discretion?" A glance at Nan. "Like Sue?"

Nan shrugged. Sue Garrie was a mouse.

Mr. Stone puckered his lips as if tasting something piquant and arched a silver eyebrow. For a second, his face was lively.

"I appreciate it anyway," he said. "I'll let you in on something. I was thinking of retiring before they threw me out. I actually feel quite well, probably better than I have in years. When does someone stop 'having' cancer anyway? Two years? Five years? It's been eighteen months since my treatment stopped and I feel fine. Oh, and . . . my marriage isn't in trouble. It's over."

That was mean, Nan thought. After all, she *hadn't* asked. But no doubt he was used to being in charge. Events had bullied him, and he was using her to dust himself off. She didn't mind, really. There was a transparency to him that she associated with all politicians, a kind of innocence. People obviously playing a deceitful game sometimes, in certain lights, looked clean; the way, on a camping trip you washed the plates with sand, what you called "dirt" at home. It was his blank face that unsettled her. Expressions that used to live there had departed. Would it stay empty, or would something else move in? Her sketchbook tugged at her arm, a dull friend, but she would take her chances with Mr. Stone.

They chatted about vitamins and Robert Ludlum. Mr. Stone adjusted his chair to a higher position and leaned back, smiling at the sky. Nan sensed she was being charmed. Flirted with, she thought, enjoying the absurdity of the idea. Zeeta had at least fifteen years on her.

The sun appeared after a few minutes. The clouds were breaking up. Sue Garrie came out of the change room and began splashing in the shallow end. Helen Brittel entered by the gate and, pretending not to notice Nan and Mr. Stone, sat down some distance away. Nan caught the senator's cocked eyebrow. Then Sue, meek and dripping, poking a towel at herself, trotted by with a fawning smile and sat down beside Helen. Nan heard bits of an anecdote about a black saleswoman with a notorious temper, and Sue's appalled "Oh . . . oh no?"'s, along with nervous giggles.

~

At the same time, Les was coming to the end of his tenure as John's fishing buddy. He had seen something of the sort on its way: the Brittels liked to "make" friends rather than find them; but he had expected them also to need to keep friends once made, and so to prefer a fade-out rather than a rift. But something happened to force the issue.

They had caught three sea trout that day, which were in the plastic pail between them. They were joking about how pleased Ron Dinkins would be – a non-fisherman who loved to scrounge extras – when something took John's shrimp and headed towards the middle of Charlotte Harbour with it.

The line sang out with a whine. John set the hook once, twice, as the nylon streamed out. Flustered, he scrambled to his feet, shooting out a leg that knocked over the shrimp bucket; for the first time, he looked crippled. He held the cork butt of the rod against his belt, unused tendons standing out along his thin forearms; his face was red. He leaned slightly in the direction away from the one the fish was running in, a spurned suggestion.

Les saw a huge grey shape, deep down in dark water, propelling itself away from the shallows where it had felt a sharp pain.

Footsteps banged on the wooden walk. Art Buck and Don Rickert had left their poles and come down to see what was happening.

"Shark, maybe?" Art Buck said, behind them.

"Gotta be," John puffed, jerking at the drag star with his thumb. "I can't even turn it." He sounded incredulous.

"Careful, J.B. That's Ron's dinner," Rickert chuckled.

"There's lots of big fish," Buck said. "A snook might be able to do that. A big one."

"I must be almost out of line," John said, trying to peer inside the reel while holding the bowed rod.

"Hey, hey," said a familiar deep voice. Les glanced aside and saw Oscar Garrie looming, looking less phlegmatic than usual, his interest piqued. *This* was evidence.

In snapping the line, the fish almost took John over the railing. He had succeeded in tightening the drag to the point where the rod was almost wrenched out of his hands. Clutching it, he gave a small yelp. Les shot out his hand and grabbed him by the belt. The cane fell into the water. He pulled John back. "Jesus Christ!" John said, staring at his reel.

Art Buck used his rod to steer the cane down the length of the pier to the shore, where Oscar Garrie could reach it. Garrie swished it back and forth in the water to get the mud off.

Les had an extra spool of line which he gave to John. The incident began to recede. Except that Les could tell something had changed. It was so strange, the quickness of it, but he felt he was right. He was being phased out. More curious than hurt, he wondered why. Was it the hand on the belt, John's momentary helplessness? Anyone would be. But John had been. An encounter with a fish like that changes the nature of fishing, the roles being played. At the same time, Oscar's sluggish personality had finally been mobilized. He was asking John questions about fishing, and John was answering them thoroughly. Les felt he was seeing the groundwork of another alliance being laid.

Later he said to Nan, who had heard all about John's "whale," "I think the Stayners are about ready for bed." Forty years before, the old bores had eventually nodded off, leaving the newlyweds alone.

Nan was in the kitchen mixing up some Quaker muffins. "I hope so," she murmured.

~

A few days later, walking home from the dock, Les saw Helen and Nan crossing the road up ahead of him. He hesitated, then called, "Hello, ladies!" Knowing John was right behind him.

The two women turned. Helen dug her elbow at Nan's side, saying something that made them both chuckle. Les shook his empty stringer. Helen laughed harder but Nan only shook her head. It struck Les that he had married the right woman.

The turtle that Les and Nan had seen before moved out of the bushes and began crossing the road. Its leathery grey legs swept out slowly from its sides as it carried itself across the road in short stages that were like successive heavings of itself. Despite its bulk, it was almost silent.

Hearing the surf sound of John's Cadillac behind him, Les moved over so that he was standing between the turtle and the car. Nan came and joined him. These actions, which in retrospect seemed so deliberate, did not feel that way at the time. The Atwaters merely gravitated to where they were needed.

The turtle had stopped. They stopped behind it.

Behind them, the Caddy's electric window whined down. John called sharply, "Helen!" Helen Brittel appeared flustered for some moments, then went to join her husband. She gave the Atwaters a wide berth, walking on the grass to avoid them. Her flip-flops smacked against her soles. The Atwaters heard a crunch of gravel as John backed up to take the other road around the palms. Nan glanced behind her and saw Helen jogging to catch up to the car. "Come on!" she heard. The door slammed.

Then the Atwaters were alone. They did not look at each other. They watched instead the turtle, which, with its limbs and head retracted, resembled more than ever an army helmet. An old grey army helmet left in the middle of the road, which it had somehow become their important task to guard. It was not necessary to ask themselves why.

Les touched the back of the turtle's shell with the toe of his shoe. Nothing happened. He touched it again. This time, the head shot out with its wet hiss.

"Oh!" Nan exclaimed as Les stepped back.

He prodded the shell again and the same thing happened, except that the hiss was more insistent and prolonged, the beak swifter.

Now Les grunted, "Oh!" Nan, annoyed with him for touching the turtle again after the first warning, said nothing.

As they stood there, in the middle of the dusty road in the pink light of the waning day, they felt a quiet victory in what had just occurred. Each, for the first time, felt that the trip might prove to be a success; that, finally, sufficient grounds had been laid down for the retirement to proceed. Each suspected the other of feeling the same sense of triumph, but they did not look at one another. It was easier to share the feeling by looking at the road.

LIBBY CREELMAN

Sunken Island

The sun fell in a yellow slant through the hemlocks and blazed my eager back as though this were its first day on earth. In a minute or two, it would travel up the oilcloth and puddle over my poached eggs, creamed corn, and sweet tea – flavours that would stay on my tongue the morning.

"Today's the day, you two," my grandmother said, her voice raspy, feeble because it was so early. "To Sunken Island and back again." She hobbled towards us from the cookstove, the sound of her slippered feet like rain pattering in a straight track across the floor.

An hour later my grandmother sat at the stern of the rowboat in a grey skirt and pale blue jersey, her crutch sticking out behind her. The boy who did the yardwork rowed.

I swam in the water beside them.

I thought of my sister Harriet slipping from the breakfast table and vanishing, mute to my grandmother's threats called out across the hillside. Her place was here, alongside me, but instead she hid beneath a cot in one of the empty cottages, her long unbrushed hair now sticky with cobwebs.

The boy pulled the oars onto his lap and sat without moving as the bow of the boat nudged Sunken Island. My grandmother exhaled cigarette smoke and said, "Well, Lucy, you've made it this far."

Sunken Island was this: a pile of algae-green rocks, a dead

island licked again and again by clear lake water. The smell that arose from it was as fishy and sour as the dish rag that hung from a single nail beneath our kitchen sink. I circled it widely, afraid to touch it with my bare skin, then began swimming back towards the green-smudge of shoreline. Silken bubbles formed, burst, and uncurled against my skin.

The rowboat followed closely. When I looked up and saw my grandmother watching me, I was not surprised. Smoke twisted out her nose as she tossed her cigarette onto the water and I imagined its sogginess, the sound it made as it sizzled on the surface of the lake somewhere near me. Suddenly, I was aware of my grandmother's deep, unmistakable unhappiness; of the fact that there was some part of her that did not, after all, want me to succeed at this test. The taste of breakfast grew stronger in my mouth. I stalled, treading the water gently, and felt the cool-ness of the lower reaches of the lake surrounding my feet.

My grandmother spoke to the boy, then bent towards me over the stern of the boat, extending her crutch for my hands to take.

"Tell me again, how it happened," Harriet said.

It was the first week of summer. Harriet and I were sitting on a bed in the sleeping cottage, watching my mother dress for a doctor's appointment. She had just come out of the lake.

"It was an accident," my mother said. "You know that, Harriet. You ask me this all the time."

My mother was putting on her bra, the way she always did, with her back to us. She fastened it at the front and then twisted it around, poking her arms through the straps and lifting the cups into place. When she turned back to us she said, "She slipped on the ice. She didn't heal well. She was young. End of story."

Then she smiled, and sat down between us, reaching out to tuck my bangs behind my ears. "Wash your hair at swimming time," she said to me, then looked at Harriet. "Both of you."

"It's a pretty dress," I told her, and silently we all looked down at it: sleeveless, with brown and orange flowers against which my mother's glossy, tanned body seemed camouflaged. She smelled fresh, of shampoo, lotion, powder, and her own still-hot skin. But it was impossible for me to decipher her odour, to pick out the parts.

The sleeping cottage was a maze of connecting rooms, dim and safe, even at midday. It was here each night that Harriet and I, washed and ready for bed, waited under plaid flannel blankets for our grandmother to come up to us.

We would hear the sound of the kitchen door squeaking as it opened then slapped shut again, and of my grandmother stepping out into the night. I would sit up and press my face to the screen and watch her where she paused below, checking her apron pockets for cigarettes. She limped the short distance towards the stairs that led up to us, then took the handrail and climbed slowly, one step at a time, carrying her crutch.

She entered the room with a hand outstretched, lurching towards one of our cots. When she sat at my side I could smell the wood and rubber of her crutch, and the smoky sweetness of her pockets.

Each night she told us the same stories she had heard as a child, in which the lake fairy, a small winged creature once seen by her own mother, frequently appeared.

"Did you see her too?" we would ask.

"No, dear, never. She's patient business."

Naturally, I searched for the lake fairy during the day, wading along the lake's edge where mysteriously there was no beach, where the slender trees seemed to sprout from the water itself. And I waited for her at night, while the wind scratched at the hemlocks above and Harriet breathed rhythmically in her sleep. I hoped she might climb the outside of the cottage and cling to the mesh of the screen windows with her tiny hands; that if asleep, I might somehow know to awake and see her there, watching us.

The stories ended when my grandmother's cigarette ash had grown long and was bending, dry and grey, above her cupped hand, and we would drift off hearing the lake lap the shore, the hot click of insects in the trees.

Harriet and I knew not to expect visitors. Outsiders were rarely welcomed by my grandmother and were allowed access to our lives only when necessary, and always with disapproval. She complained to us of the boy who came to stack the wood and rake the yard: *Why doesn't he wash his hair?* she asked us, as though such a simple act would bring him great rewards. And the woman to whom we brought the laundry: *I wish she'd purchase herself some decent clothing, get rid of those rags. Pity she can't sew.*

It was a surprise then when a charcoal-coloured Mercedes arrived one afternoon, travelling so quietly we could hear the slow crunch of its tires over the stone drive.

"Damnation," my grandmother whispered. "Here comes Carmela."

"Who's Carmela?" we asked.

Coughing, my grandmother smashed out her cigarette and pushed her crossword puzzle away.

"Who's Carmela?"

"Lucy, don't shout. She's nobody. I used to play with her. Hand me my crutch, dear. I better get out and meet her or she'll be coming in."

My grandmother moved as fast as she could, her right shoulder hooked over the top of one crutch and her longer leg hustling. I watched her go over the dirt yard that was worn down as smooth as ice, the ball of her foot on her shorter leg coasting easily across it. Sunlight came down through the tall trees, frayed and peaceful, grazing her shoulders, brown skirt, her navy blue sneakers.

Carmela stepped from her car and moved quickly when she saw that my grandmother was already outside.

They kissed, and Carmela handed her a small basket.

"I wish you wouldn't do this," my grandmother said gratefully.

Carmela was making soft clucking sounds, running her flattened palms over her skirt and blouse with a manner more ladylike than anything I'd ever seen my grandmother perform.

"Keep some for yourself," my grandmother offered. "This is too much."

"I've got plenty. Believe me. Plenty."

"You're too generous. You shouldn't bring them every year."

Carmela was looking around. Finally she spotted us, sitting on the porch floor behind the screens.

"Marigold, are those two big girls your grandchildren?"

My grandmother nodded.

"That big already? Isn't that lovely."

"They're with me for the summer."

Carmela gave my grandmother a long look. She seemed to be waiting.

"Barbara is in for an operation."

"Yes, and from what I've been hearing, Marigold, it was about time, too."

"I never see cause," my grandmother said, in a voice unsteady but familiar to me, "for turning everything into a big hurry."

Carmela gave us a brief, sympathetic look. "My niece Lizzie? You remember her, Marigold. I think it would be a lovely idea if she came out here for a while. Give you a hand. Her mother tells me she's bored silly this summer."

"Please. Don't bother with anything like that."

"Now, Marigold, I know you. It's clear you need some help around here."

"I don't need any such thing." But for a moment my grandmother would not meet this woman's eyes. It was when she smiled that I saw how angry she was.

Carmela left, and we followed my grandmother into the kitchen, curious to discover what was in the basket. She held it out to us, then drew it back when we tried to reach inside. "Every summer that damn woman brings me red raspberries. Maggoty with seeds. Ruin your teeth."

"How old's this Lizzie person?" Harriet asked.

"Set the table, girls."

Harriet grabbed the mismatched plates and glasses from the cupboard and handed them over to me without looking my way. I wanted to catch her eye but she was moving quickly, running around the table slapping down the knives, forks, and spoons.

"Put some order to it, Harriet," my grandmother corrected.

"How old is this Lizzie?" Harriet asked again, backing away from the table.

My grandmother turned wearily towards the window that looked out across the lake. "Why couldn't that woman have left us alone?"

I set the plates down carefully, rearranging the cutlery, folding the paper napkins into perfect sails and tucking them safely beneath the plates. We each had a favourite plate, even my grandmother. Harriet's was one-of-a-kind, with peach-coloured roses and faded vines, scalloped edges, and minute, delicate cracks. Mine was not one-of-a-kind. It had a vibrant red unidentified flower in the centre and was one of several that my grandmother also claimed as her favourite.

My mother's was blue, light blue and so old nothing of the original pattern could be seen. We were keeping it at the bottom of the stack until she returned.

It was hot, the day following Carmela's visit. Usually we were safe from the heat under the tall hemlocks, beside the lake. But the sun came down and found us, especially my grandmother. She easily grew weak and pink-faced on these days.

Then, mid-morning, Carmela returned with her niece, who was driving the Mercedes. She parked it far up on the dirt drive on a patch of lime green moss my grandmother preferred we never walked across.

"True to my word, Marigold," Carmela said, sailing over to us. "I've brought you some help. Lizzie loves to work."

"I just love children," Lizzie said.

We stared openly at Lizzie. She had blonde hair that looked as though someone had spent the morning brushing it, stroke after stroke after stroke. She was wearing pressed white shorts with a flowered turned-up hem, and a matching white blouse with a flowered collar and flowered turned-up sleeves. She was glamorous.

My grandmother had both crutches with her. She was sagging between them. Her hair had fallen out on her neck and her face was no longer pink, but more the colour of vanilla ice cream, like her bad leg.

"I truly do not need –"

"Don't be a goose, Marigold."

"Carmela, listen to me."

"People love to help you."

My grandmother shifted, rearranging her weight over her crutches. "This heat is merciless."

"It's the humidity," Lizzie said.

"But notice, Lizzie, how lovely and cool it is down here," Carmela said. "It's hot as the blazes in town, Marigold. You're lucky to still have this place."

My grandmother transferred one of her crutches to her other side in order to free an arm, and began patting her apron pockets. "Damn," she whispered.

"What's that?" Carmela asked.

"My cigarettes. I left them inside. Damn, and damn again."

There was a brief silence. "Good Heavens, Lizzie," Carmela said. "What are you standing there for? Go and fetch Marigold's cigarettes."

"Well, where are they?"

My grandmother hesitated. She studied Lizzie from head to toe. "On the card table, at the end of the porch," she said at last.

Lizzie trotted inside. Carmela looked relieved. "Believe me, I'll have a word with her about what's expected."

"For cripes sake, don't bother," my grandmother said, no longer looking at Carmela. She took the cigarette pack from Lizzie. Her mouth tightened around the cigarette as she lit it.

"So it's settled," Carmela said. "I'll bring Lizzie back with her things tomorrow."

My grandmother nodded. She exhaled, scanning the far shore of the lake.

Because of the heat we were allowed to go skinny-dipping that night, just before bed.

Harriet and I carried down a bar of soap and towels. Behind us, our grandmother followed, her crutches swishing against the leathery-leafed mountain laurel. When we went into the water we went carefully, not speaking, using memory to feel our way over the rocky bottom of the black water.

The lake sucked away the heat from my body and I imagined it might feel like this standing on another world, where the air might be like water, where everything might touch you in a changed but pleasant way.

I turned and searched the shore for my grandmother. The off-and-on red glow of her cigarette was the only indication that she stood there at the water's edge, disguised by vegetation and by night. Yet somehow her presence was as clear as day to me, as though her spirit were the strongest thing about her.

I knew that she would swim later, after we were asleep. She cherished her time in the water, floating on her back, her grey hair loose around her while she gazed at the sky. She was so light, she seemed almost to rest on the surface of the water without penetrating it.

But as I lay in bed that night I thought of her making her way back down to the lake, her arms hooked over the tops of her crutches, her slender arms working to carry her. I thought how strong those arms must be to have supported her for so long, yet the sight of that bend at her elbows always stirred in me a combination of feelings I didn't know how to name.

I prayed she would not slip in the dark before reaching the lake.

Lizzie was sixteen years old and there was little about her my grandmother could fault. Her clothes were not rags and she washed her hair every night in the sink. Although my grandmother repeatedly remarked how ridiculous she was not to bathe in the lake like the rest of us, in the long run I believe she was relieved to have her. The only complaint I ever heard her make about Lizzie was that she was boy-crazy.

"Like a dog in heat," my grandmother said. "Imagine a girl her age going around with a twenty-six-year-old man. It takes no stretch of the imagination to wonder why they packed her off to me."

But Harriet and I fell immediately in love with her. We marvelled as she put away her clothes.

"Shoot, this is nothing," Lizzie told us. "If you could see what's left at home. If that house burns down on me? I'll kill someone."

At night, Lizzie flew up the steps to the sleeping cottage, telling us our grandmother was too tuckered out from the day we'd given her to come up herself. I found this difficult to accept, for these were the same days we had always given her, and now she had Lizzie to help with the groceries, the laundry, the constant sweeping and mopping. Gradually, there began to awaken in me feelings of anger and resentment towards my grandmother I had never been aware of before.

Perhaps if I had complained, the response might have allowed me to see just how troubled my grandmother was that summer. Perhaps I might have even perceived – however distantly – that this was to be my last summer at the lake, that I would never hear anyone speak of the lake fairy again, never hear my grandmother's cool whispered words describing her.

"Show us your boobs," Harriet said to Lizzie the second night.

"Mind your beeswax," Lizzie returned lazily.

"I just want to see what they look like."

"You'll get your own some day."

"I want to see what they look like now."

"Show us," I begged.

"Well, all right. Turn that light off." She sounded as though she just wanted to get the thing over with. She lifted her blouse and there was her bra, edged with pretty pink lace.

"No!" Harriet said. "Your boobs."

Lizzie smirked and reached behind to unfasten her bra, just as Harriet sprung into the air and yanked the light back on. For a moment I saw swing free two white mounds with dark centres the size of quarters.

"Cheater," Lizzie said in a different voice, both tolerant and resentful. She took her time putting herself back together, then whispered, "Go to sleep."

Harriet and I lay silently in the dark. I had often seen my grandmother naked, stripping out of her wet suit after swimming. But she did not have anything like those on her chest. Her body was wrapped in thin folds that were like waves. Except for her scar, which ran deeply inwards at the top of her bad leg.

Almost every night thereafter, Lizzie crossed the room and in the dimming light exposed herself to us. Eventually she did not need to be coerced, but came to us, waiting until all that anyone could hear was the occasional buckle of a slack screen or chirp of a lone cricket in the closet, and lifted her blouse. She turned first slightly towards Harriet, then shifted back towards me, so that we were allowed the privilege of viewing her from all angles. In that just-past-dusk light, the kitchen lights coming up from the cottage below yellow and starchy, Lizzie's breasts might have been marble rather than flesh, but though Harriet asked, we were never given permission to touch them.

As she released her blouse her hands floated to her hips like discarded gloves. When I realized she was removing her bra in preparation for these visits, a strange and new excitement swept through me, as if my role was, in some way, one of complicity.

But Lizzie had a manner of exposing her body and describing details of what she and her boyfriend had done – beneath trees and bushes in broad daylight – that stilled me with a secret terror. After she left our room each night I lay awake anxiously imagining the way my own body would change, the events that could, some day, happen to me.

Lizzie knew other things too.

One night, she told us that when our grandmother was young, she had gone to university for a year studying to become a mathematician.

"A what?" I asked.

"Adding, subtracting. Aunt Carmela says she was a real hotshot brain."

"Is she still?"

"Gawd no, Lucy. Does she look like one? Too bad she went and fell down on that old ice. I bet she hates winter."

"Why would she hate winter?"

"You don't understand anything, Lucy," Harriet said.

"Aunt Carmela says she couldn't have her cake and eat it too. That's why no one in your family has a real life. Well? Take a look around you."

"I have a real life," I insisted, upset.

But Lizzie only stared at us, her expression unsettled and indulgent, her fingers restless with the hem of her blouse.

One day, towards the end of summer, Lizzie left, back to her boyfriend and her wardrobe. That evening my grandmother, Harriet and I carried birthday candles and paper baking cups down to the shore. We melted the ends of the candles and stuck them upright inside the cups, then set them in the water. My grandmother used her crutch to gently push them off, out beyond the danger of the small breaking waves.

We waited and watched, and after a while the water was lit by the yellow lights of a dozen candles heading across the lake in baking cups. Eventually most went out, either burned down or capsized, but several continued on, blinking precariously.

My grandmother whispered, "Almost all the way to Sunken Island, girls."

The following day I tried to swim to Sunken Island and back again. This time I did not stall halfway to shore, dropping my legs under me in the deep water and reaching out for my grandmother's crutch. Instead I swam with an unfamiliar determination that in itself was almost frightening enough to make me give up. But there had been something distancing me from my grandmother all summer – perhaps Lizzie's demonstrations at bedtime while my grandmother remained below, tired and worried – that allowed me now to ignore her as she sat, smoking, in the rowboat. I kept my eyes on the rim of the lake where the leafy, cool shore came down to meet the rocks, staring so hard that after a while I saw a tiny figure drifting among the trees.

I panicked, and almost stopped. Then it came to me that here, at last, was the lake fairy, just as my grandmother had described her: pretty and strong, wearing a white dress, hovering over the tops of the trees. I heard my grandmother's crutch bang loudly on the metal side of the boat, but I continued to ignore her, watching instead the lake fairy until she disappeared among the vegetation.

Finally, my feet touched the floor of the lake. In the cold

shade covering the grassless earth I looked up towards the cottages and saw that my mother had returned.

The rowboat jabbed the shore behind me and my grandmother said, "Lucy, hurry now and get a towel. You'll catch your death."

I had not seen my mother for over a month. When I went to meet her I almost didn't recognize her. I looked at her breasts, at the shape they made through her pink jersey. It was impossible to tell which one they had taken.

"I just swam to Sunken Island and back again," I told her as she swiftly wrapped a towel around me.

"Oh," she said. "I was never able to do that."

MIKE FINIGAN

Passion Sunday

Elic didn't much like Colin, but he sat with him at Mass because Colin was the only one he could let on he knew. Besides, if he wanted to become good, Colin was a good role model. Too good maybe, but . . .

"G'day," he said. They were kneeling.

Colin didn't much like Elic either, coming to Mass with the jeans on, and the black leather jacket, and black eyes, or split lips, and smelling of last night's liquor. And always with the heart on the sleeve; repentant from one end of Mass to the other, depending on the length of the homily. Anyway, you had to let him sit by you, or else face being killed as you took a shot of rum from your glass in a Legion six months to ten years from now.

"How're you t'day?"

Elic crossed himself with a thickly bandaged right hand. He loved crossing himself. He caught Colin looking.

"Sliced a tendon on a beer glass," Elic said. "I was goin' for Aubrey Boland's nose up at the Legion for the second time, but somebody held me arm back for a split second and the bastard got the glass up in front of him."

"We're at Mass," Colin whispered.

"Eh . . . yeah," Elic said, apologizing.

A cloud crossed his face and he looked soberly at Colin.

"Do yeh think there's any hope for me?"

Colin shrugged. "Go to confession. Ask Father. He's better equipped to tell you."

Elic contemplated. "I ain't Catholic, though. I don't know the rules in there."

"And you've been receiving Holy Communion!" Colin whispered sharply.

"Yeah. Well," Elic said.

"You'd better hope Father doesn't find out," Colin said.

"How's he going to find out?"

They prayed.

The pews were filling up. Elic said, "There's that Melvin Pastuck."

Melvin Pastuck was down in front, genuflecting extravagantly. On his knees, face to the ceiling, arms out in supplication. He was short and husky with a ponytail and a wiry beard. He wore a combat jacket, jogging pants, and a pair of orangey-coloured workboots.

"Coming in here, looking like that," Colin said.

"He's from Boston. Been here a couple a months," Elic said. "Did yeh ever hear tell of him?"

Colin shook his head curtly.

"Who comes to live in Glace Bay from Boston?" Elic pondered.

Colin shrugged and let on he was still trying to pray.

"He musta had people here once," Elic surmised. "Everybody used t'go teh Boston before they started goin' teh Tronno. Maybe he's lookin' for he's roots." He thought out loud, "Pastuck. Pastuck . . ."

Colin stiffened in his prayer.

"They say he thinks he's Jesus," Elic said.

Colin raised an eyebrow and studied Melvin Pastuck. "First or second coming?"

Elic didn't know.

"You have to watch the second comings," Colin said suspiciously. "The terrorists."

Elic thought and said, "You kinda gotta like 'im, though."

Colin didn't say anything.

"Those're hundred-and-thirty-five-dollar boots," Elic said.

Colin moved away an inch or two, almost imperceptibly.

Elic wondered if it was his breath. God! he was hungover. And the hand! Throb? It was like it had a heart of its own. The freezing was coming out.

What a life.

He watched Melvin Pastuck. Melvin was all caught up. There could have been no one else in the church for all Melvin knew. Elic wished he could pray like that. He wished he could be connected to God like that. But there wasn't much chance of it today. Not with a hangover like this. And it was no sense in saying it was the last one. No sense at all. One small comfort Elic took from getting older was that he became wise enough to know he was going to be stupid no matter how smart he was. The first thousand hangovers came with a vow to never drink again. Now they came alone, the good devil that hangs over the guy's right shoulder in the cartoons and TV shows finally killed off by relentless attacks of fun. And they stayed longer.

Before the priest got going, he got everyone to say hello to the people near to them. When he first started coming to Mass, Elic felt uncomfortable with this practice. He forgot about it going in and always wound up shaking hands with people he felt uncomfortable with, people who he knew didn't like him or approve of him and who smiled meanly at him. And he felt conscious of the fact that he was there by himself. But after a few times in he remembered to find somebody to sit with who he knew a little at least, a peer of some degree. And the best he could do was Colin. He would have sat with Melvin Pastuck, but Melvin was too involved with God all the time. So he sat with Colin and didn't feel like he was sticking out like a sore thumb. He shook hands with everyone around like he was a regular part of things. He enjoyed shaking hands. "G'day," "How's she goin'?" In time he learned just to say, "Good morning." This morning he felt lucky, for when he turned around there were two fine-looking young ones sitting behind him, all wide-eyed and scrubbed clean and smelling like a spring morning. They were eager to say hello too. "Good morning," he said with a charming smile full of strong white teeth. He couldn't fool himself. He knew his smile was a charmer. And his leather jacket. "Hi!" they said, giggling to each other. They were a little younger than he expected.

They were standing and standing. There was a crew doing The Passion. Colin was upset that Jimmy Ratchford was still Jesus after four years. "They should give someone else a chance up there," he said. "They're nothing but a clique."

Jimmy Ratchford was bored, it was plain. He missed his cue after Simon Peter cut off the guard's ear. He was in another world. Everyone waited and waited.

"And Jesus slept," Colin said, fanning himself with a bulletin. "Clique."

"Those three old ones," Elic whispered during the collection. He was nodding toward the MacInnises, old Angus and his two sisters, Mary and Alice. "They're always here," he said.

Angus sat to the right of them. They were all big and granite-looking in their grey outfits. They all had white hair. They lived up on Swallow's Hill in the same house. They'd been there forever. They came from Scotland, some people said, and cleared the Hill when it was just woods. They never married. Any of them. But nobody seemed to take it as odd. "They're all wrapped up in their prayer beads," Elic said. "It's like they washed up on the beach, tangled up in somebody's lines."

"They never miss a single Mass," Colin said. "They come every day, Father says. They're old church."

"They're like three big rocks," Elic said. They seemed mysterious, biblical somehow, not that Elic had ever read *The Holy Bible* thoroughly enough to know what he meant when he said that. Not that he'd ever read it at all. Most of what he knew about Christianity came from his Uncle John, whose religion consisted of a pocketful of mixed scriptural quotations that he used indiscriminately and usually in self-defence; a love of God, a contempt for holy rollers – especially Roman Catholic Holy Rollers – and a condescending tolerance for anybody who wasn't Roman Catholic. The old ones conveyed the essence of the Roman Catholic Church for Elic though.

"I'm thinkin' about becomin' a Catholic," he said. "Mainly because a them. I can feel their faith. They're solid. I'd like to be solid like that." Elic looked around at the statuary and the relics, at the pews and the stained-glass windows. He inhaled and exhaled deeply through his nose. "I like the whole thing," he said, rhetorically. "The beads, the crucifixes, the holy water. The saints. I love the saints. Even the plastic Jesuses and the Virgin Mary lamps." At my church, Elic thought, they're always putting that stuff down. But it seemed a way to keep God on your mind all the time. Doing the beads and reading about somebody thanking St. Jude for the favours in the classifieds. And Mass every day. It kept a person in touch. At my church, he thought, you get God for an hour on Sunday morning and then everyone goes for tea in the basement and talks about how nice the service was. It's not even Mass! It's a service! *Wasn't that a nice service, dear? It was. It was so nice.* All the old ones with the blue hair comin' up and askin' yeh if yeh want more tea. He hated nice. If there was one thing he couldn't stand, it was nice. I'd rather have the shit beat outta me, he thought. And after the social, everyone goes home. They turn out the lights and leave God in the basement with a half a package of Peak Freans and a cup of cold tea. See yeh.

"What I like about the Catholics," Elic whispered as best he could to Colin, though he was not good at whispering as his deep voice would cut in and out conspicuously, "is that they aren't nice. No offence."

"They've sunk a lot into this place, I'm told," Colin said, still on the subject of the old ones. "They've got a few bucks. They're holding the place up, they say." Then Colin wished he hadn't said that. He pictured Elic drunk, trying to break in. "*Shh* now. We shouldn't be talking. We're getting the eyes."

"Did you ever talk to them?" Elic said.

"No," Colin said shortly.

The ushers were coming. Elic fished through his pockets with his good hand. He withdrew a five and a twenty. He put the twenty in. He looked at Colin. "I'm not showin' off," he said. "I have to stop spending so much on the booze, so I'm doing this for spite. It's terrible when you think about it. I'll look at a forty-dollar pair of pants for a week. I'll go to the store and look at them and I'll go back and look at them again a few days later and finally, a week later, I won't buy them because they're forty dollars. But then I'll spend seventy-five on the way home in the Legion without a moment's notice. Funny, ain' it? I really have to get me priorities straight."

People were turning around and looking.

"*Shhh*, will yeh?" Colin said.

Mildred MacIntyre, a white-haired, little old ex-nun, turned around from the pew in front with her eyes hot and gave a stifled "*Sh!*" Elic flushed and Colin caught another whiff of liquor and leather coming from him. Mildred MacIntyre gave him the hot look too. Does she think it's me? he thought.

Elic leaned forward and said to her in his broken whisper, "I was just tellin' him, 'In My house there are many mansions.'" It was the only quote he could think of. His Uncle John used it all the time.

"You were not," Mildred whispered, and she almost withered in the fire of Elic's breath. "You were talking about the liquor! At Mass!" she added. "My God!" she whispered. "Is there no place sacred any more?" She stuck an elbow into her husband Tom's ribs – Tom, whom Elic recognized from the Legion and who was trying desperately to mind his own business. Tom didn't frequent the Legion much, but when he was there he made good use of it. And, according to Stan Graves the taxi driver, Tom called most of his liquor in at home and received it through the missing board in the back of his coal barn facing the back road away from his house. Elic watched Tom's red/blue profile, but Tom didn't turn around or even acknowledge the elbow. He knew he couldn't cast any stones.

"You're right, Sis . . . eh . . ." Elic flushed again. Everyone still called her "Sister" even though she'd left the nuns before he'd been born. "Eh . . . Mrs. MacIntyre. I was. I'm . . . I'm a wicked alchy," he said, surprised at the sound of his own words. "I was hopin' to straighten up and fly right. Coming here would help me start, I figured." And he smiled cheerfully.

"You talk as though you're proud of it," Mildred said. "Now, I can hear every word you're saying!"

Elic reddened at the rebuke. And then, having said what he just said, he suddenly felt ill with a commitment he hoped he hadn't really made. Had he just said he was an alcoholic? Did he imply that he was going to quit drinking? No booze? Ever again? He felt weak. He started to feel what he thought might be a panic attack. Or claustrophobia. Saying the words made them much more real. I'm an alchy, he thought. Am I really? He began to take stock of his life then and there.

Who are you to be looking down the side of your nose at me, yeh witch, Colin thought. You who gave it all up for the flesh. Though why – he looked quickly at Tom, who seemed to know that he was being looked at – I can't imagine. I wouldn't be turning around at all if I was her. Does she really think I smell of that? I'll have to talk to her alone after Mass. This guy. Jesus! Surely she knows I wouldn't be hanging around the likes of him.

"On the night he was betrayed . . ." Father began, consecrating the host.

Elic hunched up his shoulders, feeling a chill. You come lookin' to straighten out . . . he thought. And then the swimming sensation washed over him again and carried his thoughts away on its tide. His concentration was down to ten-second spurts. Christ on the cross. The candles. The altar servers. One of them looked a bit old for an altar server. Aubrey Boland on the floor beside the pool table looking up in terror and madness, a broken nose, blood everywhere. The sweet Keri Swan, Elic's potential woman, somewhere in the background, screaming. Hitting the beer glass; the funny feeling of being sliced open. The hot feeling. Throwing up. The lovely Keri Swan throwing up too somewhere in the background. The effects of the severed tendon; he could bend his finger but couldn't straighten it back up; going to the Glace Bay General Emergency Room, meeting up again with Aubrey Boland there. The nurses threatening to call the cops. Having a smoke with Aubrey. Laughing like hell. And then getting into it again over who won the fight until the nurses dragged them off into separate rooms. The doctor all pissed off and disgusted. C'mon now, Elic. You're at Mass. Christ on the cross. The choir singing. They were great. Bobby

Lowe hitting the odd bad chord, though, on the guitar. He looked pretty bad. The hair all over the place. No whites to the eyes. The tie crooked. He could sing though. And better when he was rumsick. God! Rumsick! The liquor everywhere! It did something to his vocal chords, though, the day after. Lowered his voice. Bobby'd been in the band last night. He was in about three bands, Bobby. It was killin' him. He played, he drank. The choir director was givin' him murderous looks. No wonder. Bobby was after him to join. Maybe he'd see. But he might have to become a Catholic first, probably. He'd see. It'd be a good way to meet that Sandy Aucoin too. She had that voluptuous smile. She weighed a few pounds, but that smile. And when he made it to Mass, he was always catching her looking. He should really be settling down too. He was getting too old for this kind of goin's on. She was attractive, by God. What a smile. He should see Bobby about the two of them joining AA too. A twinge in the stitched tendon. It was going to put him off work in the pit. He'd probably get the insurance, though. Nah. Light duty most likely. Sweepin' floors on the surface or something. The boys'll be sayin' he did it on purpose. Maybe he should have put the five in the collection instead of the twenty, just in case. What do these priests make a year anyway? Never mind money. All the money in the world was no good if you couldn't get laid. C'mon now, Elic. It's Mass you're in now. C'mon! That slow dance with the sexy Keri Swan last night. Keri Swan . . . *ohhh my God* . . . Keri Sw– Married though. If you call that married. The husband home four months a year maybe. Terrible thoughts now to be thinking in church! Keri Swan. She was lonely, you could tell. All tender and soft. It was like falling. Man! You don't want to be thinkin' . . . And us feelin' no pain. "On the Dark Side of the Street" playing too. The perfect waltz. God knows what would've happened if not for Aubrey Boland cutting in. God. There'd a been bigger fish to fry than a sliced tendon. Maybe he was a drunk, but he wasn't yet an adulterer. Fish. That'd be nice now. A good feed a Phil's Fish and Chips. What time does Phil's open on Sundays? Maybe he could get a nice seafood platter and a beer after Mass. No. No beer. That's it for the beer.

"'. . . take this, all of you and . . .'"

"What time does Phil's open on Sundays?" Elic asked Colin. "*Sh!*"

On the way up for Holy Communion, Elic watched nervously. He could never remember how it was done exactly, or if he'd done it right the last time. He was trying to see around people. Was there a proper hand you took it in? Wasn't there this religious disgust of the left hand? Wasn't it the sign of The Devil or something if you were left-handed? Some people just had it put on their tongue. No. He wouldn't do that. God knows what the priest might see in there, let alone smell. Then he remembered that he only had the one good hand today anyway. The left hand. They'd have to understand. He turned his attention to the wine and watched how that was done. Should he go for the wine? Maybe not. It was optional. Lots of alcoholics didn't go. But it's Christ, he thought.

Somehow, Colin had gotten ahead and was talking to a young, attractive woman in front of him. His face was scarlet over her shoulder. There was no mistaking the anger that flashed in his eyes. They all kept proceeding down the aisle, one person at a time, and then the woman turned around and parted from the line before she got to the priest. Her head was bowed and she was crying but trying not to be noticed. Colin didn't follow her, or even watch her go. He stepped up and received the host.

Elic thought he saw a suspicious look on Father's face when it was his turn.

"Body of Christ."

"Thanks."

"Pardon?"

Elic went red instantly. "Thanks," he said.

"That's *Amen*."

"That's right, too."

The bread and the wine filled him. It worked every time. Even though he wasn't Catholic.

Elic knelt in his pew. Colin was deep in prayer already. He wanted to pray, too. He tried. He hoped the Communion would help him. But he still couldn't concentrate. He was too hung over. Bloody hangovers! Would he ever learn? Was there no hope? He prayed for hope but his mind kept flipping through thoughts like it was flipping through the Canadian Tire catalogue. The Communion would have to do.

Jesus Christ, Jesus Christ, Jesus Christ, he thought. One of these days I'm going to come in here clean, and I'll pray up a storm. Help me come in clean, will yeh, piece a trash that I am?

Elic didn't know if he should mention the woman to Colin or not. But it was driving him crazy. He posed the question five or six different ways before he found a way comfortable enough to voice. "Was that woman all right?" he asked.

"That depends," Colin said directly. "She is. But she probably doesn't feel all right. She's a divorcée and married again outside the church. She's not to go for Holy Communion. She's home from Toronto and figured nobody knew." Colin saw the indignation rise up in Elic's eyes and he sensed it wasn't at the woman. "You can't fool around with Holy Communion," he said and Elic felt the universal accusation. "I saved her from hypocrisy, and from committing a terrible sin whether you like to believe that or not. Being a Catholic is not all roses and saints, you know. It's not, as you say, about being nice."

At the end of Mass, everyone was going up to the altar to get a palm frond. There was a smaller chapel inside the church, Elic knew, where people went to light vigil candles and to pray. He went in to light a candle and hoped that that would make up for his inability to pray. Melvin Pastuck had been there and was coming out. He had a breadbag with him that held a sponge soaked in what Elic learned was holy water. Melvin came toward him smiling, stopped and knelt down in front of Elic and began to rub Elic's shoes with it. Elic was embarrassed but he didn't have the nerve to walk away from him.

Melvin looked up from the floor with crazy, intense green eyes, smiling. He patted the sponge on Elic's trouser legs lightly. "The Lord says do this," he said. "It's anointment for you."

"The Lord does?" Elic asked in a slightly patronizing tone, chuckling nervously.

"You have a long way to go," Melvin Pastuck said. He smiled like he was looking down knowingly on everyone and everything.

Colin came in and saw. He'd been out talking to Mildred MacIntyre. "Is that holy water? Where did you take that from? Don't you put . . ."

"I know where you live," Melvin Pastuck said, the smile still crazy but now subtly malicious.

Outside, Aubrey Boland was going by with the broken nose. He spotted Elic on the church steps. He held up his right hand and wrung it, pretending to cry, mocking Elic's pain of last night.

Elic screwed up a fist. Thought. And let it go. "Ah, the hell with him," he said to Colin, but Colin was up on the top step with Father.

JANE EATON HAMILTON

Territory

My husband's idea of bliss is to be able to go back to when we first met, when he was a man and I was a woman. We weren't kids, not by then; we were into our late twenties. I was a veterinary assistant and Luke was a clerk at A+B Sound. Then I decided to go into medical school, a six-year commitment, and Luke, later when I was into my residency and had some earning power, decided to try his hand at poetry.

He tells me that if I had never met Holly, things would be fine.

"Define fine," I reply. Our marriage was not without problems, common though they were, even before this started. Luke forgets this. Luke denies this.

He says, "You'd still be a woman."

What am I supposed to answer to that? "I'm still a woman," I say.

It used to be that Luke and I hardly ever fought, but now Luke has been asked to do the impossible – give me up, and it doesn't look good on him. The quiet, unassuming man that he was – the man on whom I could count, no matter what – has gone into hiding, and this man who picks on me has taken his place, wearing Luke's slightly shabby clothes, using Luke's soft voice. I can rise to his bait or ignore him. There isn't a third choice.

It is very hot out. Luke hates the heat as much as Holly loves it. Holly's out of town, though, in her own, more severe heat wave in New York, where she has gone to teach. We don't get a lot of hot, hot weather here; the last time Holly called, she said she was sorry she was missing it. She said she missed *me*.

43

Luke spends his days in the living room in the purple velour rocker he loves, writing his odd, circuitous poetry. Luke writes exclusively in pencil; he shields the page if I come in the room, or even if I'm just passing by the glass doors. I can hear him mutter and often he balls up mistakes and tosses them like lightweight basketballs toward the trash can across the room. Sometimes when he's gone out, I unfold these sheets, but they don't say much. *A blue apple sits on the dresser*, one said, with the word "dresser" scratched out and replaced by "toilet."

Neither of us knows what the other one is thinking these days. Luke doesn't understand why this happened to me and, really, neither do I.

I go reluctantly. I go, but I go reluctantly. Luke thinks that I ought to have known before I married him. Maybe I should have. But having a crush on my Grade 5 teacher and admiring women's backs weren't enough warning.

I bite my lip. My pager shrills. I've been on call a lot for the past nine months. I say, "I'll just call the service." I say, "Hon."

I wait a minute, scrutinizing him. Luke's only thirty-seven, but his hair is more than half grey. Hair is an issue between us. I wish he would shave more often; I hate the black whiskers that bristle out from his white, white chin.

Luke wants more from me, some reaction, a fight.

The call isn't serious. A baby with a fever of ninety-nine degrees, a cough. After I hang up, I think of Holly, of, for some reason, the scar on her belly from her hysterectomy.

Finally I go back to Luke, put flint in my voice, and say, "People aren't as bad as you think they are." I mean Holly isn't. I mean I'm not.

Luke lifts his face from where he's staring at *Newsweek* magazine. All the anger is drained from it. His expression is lonely and sad, sad and somehow terrible. His green eyes are moist. He looks like he's lost his best friend.

We got married nearly nine years ago, in March. We had very different ideas about our lives even then. I thought I might want to go back to school to become a vet, while Luke was happy with his job at a music store. Last year, Luke suggested that maybe for our tenth anniversary we should go to Vegas, renew our vows at a drive-in Elvis chapel; it was after I told him about what I called my proclivities.

Luke didn't say anything. It was impossible to read his expression. "Why did you want me to know?" he finally asked.

"I told you so we'd have an honest marriage."

"I don't want an honest marriage," Luke said. He combed his hair with his hand. "What I want is a heterosexual wife."

I have a patient whose husband of fifty-four has Alzheimer's. He orders items by mail order when her back is turned: a silk suit, an ant farm. Although he was never a violent man, now, in his decrepitude, he hits her. I advised her to send him into a nursing home, but she shook her head. "He's my husband," she told me firmly, rubbing a bruise on her arm. "I took vows."

When we met, Holly was already dating. For the first while, I didn't say much about it. Holly would come to me weary from being up too late with Gloria, and I, tired from a rotation in the emergency room, sleep-deprived myself, wouldn't say anything. Sometimes Holly fell asleep in the middle of sex. Finally, I confronted her. "It bothers me, you know, this thing you have going with Gloria."

Holly answered with an empathetic half-smile, half-frown.

"It really does," I said, adding a bit of firmness.

Holly said, "Poor sweetie." She got up, pulled me close and held me.

"It isn't that simple."

A week or so later, emboldened because we'd just made love, I said, "Why do you keep on with her?"

That's when Holly told me their sex was out of this world. That's when she also said, "Not to put too fine a point on it, but you're married."

"But Luke and I aren't sexual," I burst. "I gave that up the first time you touched me."

"No," Holly said slowly, pulling away and lying back, hands behind her head, "you're right. I can't keep on making love to both of you."

I was uplifted.

She turned her head to face me, eyes round and too big. She said, "I can't have sex with you any more. Not while I'm still with Gloria."

I felt a stab of pain under my breastbone that I couldn't medically explain. I said, "You tell me you're in love with me. So why? Why won't you leave her?"

"For what?" Holly asked, her brows lifting.

I looked at her and she repeated it.

"For what?" she said. "A married woman?"

Luke and I have a Saturday-morning ritual. Whether or not I'm on call, Luke shoots out to the stores on West Fourth Avenue, early, then meets me in the kitchen with newspapers, coffee, and croissants. He calls these our "companionable hours." They're sweet hours because we don't have to talk. The curtains are parted and the windows cracked to the rain or sun. We do no more than rustle the news.

I am easier to live with now, Luke admitted a couple of weeks ago, because I am not as unhappy. I used to think that if he couldn't be a woman, the least he could do was be perfect. Since Holly, something's loosened.

In bed last night, I turned on my side away from Luke. I do this night after night, shiver to the furthest edge of the mattress hoping he won't want sex. But last night everything about him seemed familiar and comforting. His size, his scent, the sound of each short breath. The room was still and dark.

"Luke?" I said.

"Honey?"

"It's like I'm an alien," I said finally, rolling over. "You know what Holly says? She says I make love like a man."

I couldn't really see my husband, but I could sense him poised and waiting.

I said, "She says I'm goal-oriented."

Luke told me he didn't want to hear this.

"I want to stay with you," I said. "I don't want to be a lesbian."

Luke sighed heavily. "So give her up," he said, and I heard desperation subdued in his voice. "That's all you have to do."

Nobody said anything for the longest time, then he said, "C'mere."

I snuggled close and dropped my head into the crook of his shoulder.

In Ontario, where I joined Holly for the first leg of her trip and we had the privilege of nights together, six of them, she always cuddled up to me. It confused me. I didn't understand who was supposed to be the man and who the woman. Holly called this butch and femme, or top and bottom, and she said she was femme through and through. I, on the other hand, was butch. "Baby butch," she said, teasing me. "But all butch."

I stroked the hair on Luke's chest for a minute, thinking instead about Holly's soft skin, the gentle swell of her breasts. I cried out, "Can't I just be me?"

"I'll let you," Luke whispered solemnly, holding tight. He kissed the top of my head.

"No," I said abruptly, pulling away. I sat up fast. "Don't," I said.

"Don't what?" Luke asked, angry now, grabbing my arm. "You're my wife."

"I love you," I said helplessly.

"Then love me," he said, "love me." His hand tightened. He said, "Please."

"Let go," I said, and shook him off.

"You don't want that," Luke said, choked, but he loosened his grasp.

I said, "Luke, I think I should move out."

Before Holly left on her trip, her younger daughter, Lindsay, left a message on our machine asking if I had a blood pressure cuff she could borrow for medical day at school. It was a late day at the clinic. I slouched home, and Luke, who'd made us a tuna casserole, mentioned the message. I'm ashamed to admit I stopped, fork halfway to my mouth, took the stairs two at a time and hit Play on the answering machine.

The truth is that I should have known better. Holly was, as I knew perfectly well, only out with Gloria at an hour's dance class.

When Holly, uncomfortable after she and Gloria came in and found me there, slipped downstairs to tend to her older daughter, leaving us alone, Gloria said, "This is fucking weird."

Which is pretty well what Luke said, too, later after Holly walked me to my car and I drove home.

Luke was at that juncture my point man, the spouse to whom I brought my anecdotes and confusions.

It is the first morning since we bought our house that we've missed our Saturday-morning croissants. Luke won't talk to me. Luke is in the living room with the glass doors shut. I slip out and go pick up pastries myself, along with a copy of *The New York Times*, but when I get them home, Luke is gone.

Last night Luke said that if I was going to leave him, he should keep the house and I should support him. He's losing everything, isn't he? Isn't he?

Luke's idea is to turn the clock back.

I've been jogging a lot. It keeps me relatively healthy – a plus for a doctor – and relatively sane. When I'm jogging under the chins of the mountains along Jericho Beach, cut off from urbanity, I feel washed, clean. But just as often I run at the cemetery nearer our home, stopping sometimes to wipe my face and read the oldest gravestones, thinking about the diseases that used to eradicate whole families. My wedding certificate says I'm Catholic, but I'm actually agnostic after six years in medicine.

There is a part of me that resists this change because it is not what I imagined; I thought women's relationships would be trouble-free. I put lesbians on pedestals.

Holly was Luke's friend first. He introduced us. He came home from campus saying he'd been to a reading and met this lesbian who'd be happy to talk to me about my feelings if I'd only call her. Luke encouraged me to call her. I want that understood. Luke encouraged me.

When I was through med school and into my residency and we finally had a bit of money, I thought I could make myself better by fixing my environment. We had a house full of hand-me-down furniture – a couch, a piano, a coffee table – pieces friends had stored with us after various of their moves but never retrieved. I thought if we could only furnish our house, we'd also furnish ourselves with a good marriage. My feelings for women would just disappear.

We haunted the antique stores along Main Street. We found one shop, Sofa So Good, that had a couch and two matching chairs for just $800. Having been told that it was the way to suss out quality furniture, Luke hefted them; he could barely lift them from the floor. That meant the wood frames were solid and sturdy. Tina, the shopkeeper, was happy to refurbish them for us. Each chair, completely stripped, rebuilt, and reupholstered, would cost $600. We could afford that, just, but couldn't afford to have the couch done, too.

When we took the delivery of the chairs, I wept. Having been weighted down in the store, they were now as light as feathers. The old fabric hadn't been taken off at all – we could feel it underneath the new fabric, which was carelessly applied. We called Tina to take delivery of our couch. She told us it was in storage and we'd have to pay another $300 to retrieve it.

Sofa So Good closed down overnight; Tina moved to Vancouver Island. We were stuck with about $200 worth of substandard chairs for the whopping price of $2,000.

I answer the door to find Luke's lesbian friend Sylvia.

"Luke's not here," I say automatically, stiffening. The last time I saw Sylvia was during a kayaking trip earlier this year. I wasn't sexual with Holly yet, but I knew I wanted to be. I didn't want to be taken as straight, as a wife, when I was actually, I thought, just like Sylvia and her girlfriend. It embarrassed me. But, faithful to Luke, I was unable to say a word.

"I came to see you," she says, grinning over white, bell-shaped teeth.

I don't answer. Luke has said that he wants me to stay away from Sylvia; he worries I'll sleep with her. Or that Holly will.

She says, "Luke told me."

I look past her as if Luke might be there, home from wherever he's gone to lick his wounds – the poker club, maybe – but all I see is how the paint on the porch is wearing down to the old wood, how the lawn needs cutting and how messy the rose-bushes are. Finally, I ask Sylvia in.

"Well," I say when we're at the table with sweating glasses of lemonade.

Sylvia smiles. She says, "I had no idea when we were kayaking. I didn't have a clue. Luke says he knew."

I wait. I trail my finger through a milk spill and don't look up. I brought two cups of coffee home. When I discovered Luke had gone out, I drank mine sitting here, reading the *Book Review*, weeping. *The New York Times* is still scattered over the tabletop.

"Is this too strange?" Sylvia asks. "Me being here?"

"It's strange," I agree.

"Because I'm Luke's friend?"

I reach out and riffle a newspaper folded to the sports section. I shrug.

"Look," Sylvia says. "Dory left a marriage to come to me. Dory had a husband. I wanted to let you know that."

I glance quickly up and back down.

"I know what you're going through," Sylvia says.

I make a sound. I say, "Luke wouldn't like this."

"Why not?" Sylvia asks.

I notice Sylvia's breasts are extremely large. Then I notice them medically and wonder if she's ever considered a reduction.

Sylvia says, "Luke came over while you were away. When Dory asked him where you were, he said, and I quote: 'She's in Ontario with her lesbian lover.'" Sylvia laughs and says it again: "Lesbian lover."

I don't know how to respond. Answers tumble through my brain, such as, Holly is not my lesbian lover. Although she is. Such as, We were not in Ontario. Although we were. But what I finally say is, "Oh."

Sylvia says, "Doesn't it make Holly sound a hundred feet tall?"

"Luke's in a lot of pain," I say. "He doesn't deserve this, Sylvia." I stare out of the window at our chipped, yellow shell windchimes. Holly has tuned ones. Once as she kissed my neck, they rang out baroque, like a vibraphone. I sigh and add, "Neither does Holly. For that matter, poor Holly. She thinks I'll love her and leave her. She keeps her distance because she thinks I'm fly-by-night."

Sylvia says, "Luke says you've known you were gay for years."

"But maybe Holly's right," I say. "Maybe I'm just using her to bring me out."

I remember an anecdote Holly told me about a friend of hers who'd spent a night with a married woman. The married woman woke in the morning, rose from bed, and walked accidentally into the closet.

"Heh," Sylvia says, and reaches to take my hand.

I blink at her, pull away.

Holly's house is a large, blue-shaked place in the south city. I'd been at one of her readings and I'd made that first excruciating call to her that landed us in a greasy-spoon restaurant together, but I hadn't seen her house until the night she asked us both to dinner. To eat what she called "grunt."

"Grunt?" I asked Luke when he told me that she'd called. I didn't understand that I was attracted to her at that point; I just knew my heart began to pound when her name was mentioned. My face felt hot.

"She hates to cook," he said. Then he said, "Her stepson's coming and she needs foils."

"Stepson?" I asked, intensely curious. How could a lesbian have a stepson?

"Her ex-girlfriend's son."

"Oh," I said.

Luke and I don't have children and don't want any. That Holly had two of her own – and then this sort of third – intrigued me. Plus, she was an author. I'd been reading her when Luke was out, staring at her author photographs on back flaps.

Her house was large, light, airy yet still cosy. She used soothing colours. She had framed black-and-white photographs of women all over her walls.

The stepson, who'd showed up earlier to cadge money, didn't appear. The dinner was a lot less than good. The kids took their plates into their rooms while we ate. All I kept wishing was that Luke wasn't with me, that Holly didn't know me first – only – as Luke's wife.

In Toronto, Holly took me to the Pride Parade. I was scared; I thought my parents might see me on national TV and know I was a lesbian. Before the parade started, sitting at a restaurant called The Dundonald, a woman asked what I do for a living.

"I'm a physician," I admitted reluctantly. Most lesbians, I'd noticed, didn't seem to be much of anything, professionally speaking.

"She brought me her lab coat," Holly said, and wiggled her eyebrows.

This got hoots from the assembled women.

"Well," I said, "I did bring my stethoscope."

Holly said, "And a speculum, too."

Someone said, "Ohlala!" and everyone laughed.

One woman sobered and said, "My father was a doctor. He got called to the hospital one night when we were playing Concentration and I said to my mother, 'Why can't Daddy just let them die?'"

"No kidding," someone else said. "I hate doctors."

I looked out at the milling streets. In the hour since we'd arrived on Church Street, I'd seen men in pants with bare bottoms, men in drag, women topless, and plenty of TV cameras.

In Ontario, Holly said, "I'm scared to be in love with you."

"Why?" I asked.

Holly shrugged. "Someone will get hurt."

"I'm worried too," I admitted.

"But I am in love with you," she said. "I just don't know what I want to do about it."

I said, "I'm really not sure if I love you."

Holly looked at me. "Oh, you love me," she said definitely, then laughed, a short, barking laugh.

"I know you're in love with me," she said. "But I don't even want to be involved. And I don't want to hurt Gloria."

"We're involved," I said, wounded.

Holly sighed.

"I can't be with you if you keep on with Gloria," I told her.

"No," Holly said. "I realize that."

"Do you?" I pressed.

"Yes," she said. "I do know that much."

It was hard to do, but I asked if she loved Gloria.

"Very much," Holly said, and my heart sank. She reached and took my hand. She looked at it a moment, patted it, and said, "But I'm *in* love with you. When I look at you I see white picket fences. The whole shebang." She stroked the back of my hand with her thumb, absently. "Except I feel vulnerable and don't like it. Except that I like being alone. Except what if I screw it up? I have kids. I don't have much time. I'm distracted and busy and I love to fuck women."

Waiting a beat, bravely, I grinned and said, "Me, too."

"And what about Luke?" Holly asked.

On the phone from New York, Holly and I catch up on mundane things, my practice, her students. Then she says, "I really love you. I wrote Gloria."

Luke, from the kitchen, calls out that a coon is washing its paws on the back stairwell. He came home near dinnertime and said he'd won about $400, but other than that, we haven't spoken. He shouts, "It's been in the garbage! Hurry up!" Instead of getting off the phone, I relay what he's said to Holly and she says, "There's plenty of roadkill in N.Y. state. I've seen raccoons and squirrels and skunks. Opossums."

She says, "Why do more animals get killed on eastern highways?"

I say, "I love you."

There's a silence. Then, quietly, Holly says, "I'm so very glad that you do."

After a minute, I say, "You really wrote to Gloria?"

Holly says, "I broke it off."

"I'm happy," I say. I consider telling her that Luke and I are breaking up. But it's too hard. Instead I say, "I'd better go."

"Is Luke hovering?" Holly asks.

Luke is hovering at every moment whether he's there in the room or not, because I conjure him. He's there telling all our friends about me. Or there sitting with the lights out, morosely, a magazine unread in his lap. Or there with a paintbrush, climbing up a ladder to touch up our window sills. Or there writing poems about cuckolded husbands.

As Holly is on the east coast writing stories about women in love with married women and how married women will – it's inevitable – let them down.

As I am listening carefully to the lungs of children and, in one boy's case, ordering X-rays that won't be good.

I clear my throat. I say, "It's just hard to talk now."

"He's there, isn't he? In the room?"

"No, but –"

Holly sighs. "Is he okay?"

"He says he's an orange and I'm not leaving him for another orange, I'm leaving him for an apple, so –"

"Are you leaving him?" she breaks in to ask.

I backtrack, just not ready. "I meant emotionally."

"Oh," she says. Then she says, "He makes it sound like an apple doesn't really count."

"He just needs it known there's no trouble between us."

"Right," Holly says, sounding skeptical.

"Are you mad?"

"I'm not mad," Holly says.

"Are you mad? You sound mad."

"I'm fine."

"Are you fine?"

"Didn't I just say I was fine?"

I say, "Okay, okay, you're fine. That's good. Because everyone else I talked to today was sick."

Holly laughs.

"Even Luke's sick. He has a headache that won't quit."

"I don't want to talk about Luke," Holly says.

"No, me either."

"Well," Holly says.

"Well," I say, and tangle the phone cord around my fingers.

I go out to sit with Luke on the back stoop. "Look," he says, pointing. "One's going up that tree."

I say, "That was Holly on the phone."

"And how is Holly?" he asks tightly. I really don't know how I expect him to behave.

"Fine," I say.

"Whatever," Luke says.

The coon is up a peach tree that badly needs pruning. Everywhere I look, I can see detritus, even though the yard isn't well lit. It's still exceedingly hot. I wipe sweat from my brow. I can see our recycling pile and the spilled garbage. I can see strips of white paint peeling from the side of the garage. There are parts of several bicycles Luke is mucking with. The night is too warm, but I wrap my arms around myself, feeling chilled. I look up at the sky. The only ritual that Holly and I have so far is trying to share the perfect sunset. Trying to find a dusk where the horizon colours dazzle and the sky above flushes a perfect shade of indigo. Tonight's sunset is long past. The sky is impenetrable.

"Look," Luke says. "It's coming down. Don't move."

I watch a rotund shape shimmy backward down the peach trunk, pause, then skitter toward the house.

"There's a litter, too," Luke whispers. "Watch."

I think about Holly. When she was small, she adopted three abandoned coon kittens. They slept in bed with her. In the morning they followed her down the stairs to the kitchen where she made Pablum. She sat with them while they ate on the grass. I think about the broken blood vessels on her neck, how one raccoon, the smallest, Benjamin, suckled her as if her skin was a nipple. I don't tell this to Luke. I just sit beside him watching the coon and her young scoot in a line across our yard to the bottom porch step. Luke's put out cat chow. I listen to the coons trill, watch them stand on their hind legs to wash the kibble. I wonder if Holly's coons tried to wash Pablum.

Then Luke says, "I shouldn't encourage them."

We haven't had dinner. Nobody thought to cook. I go inside and bring back the croissants I bought this morning. I didn't wrap them properly; they're a little stale. When we finish them, I fish in my pocket and bring out a piece of paper.

I start to read.

Luke interrupts me.

"It's your poem. Be quiet. It's lovely." It is lovely. I read and read until I come to the end. It's a poem about loss. I fold it up when I'm through. Luke isn't looking at me. I touch his arm. "You wrote it for me, didn't you?"

Luke sighs. The mother coon chitters. Luke takes the paper from me. "A poet by the name of Thom Gunn wrote that."

"Oh," I say.

My beeper goes. The coons don't seem to mind the noise. It's the service again, giving me a number that seems vaguely familiar. I bring the phone out onto the porch and return the call. It seems the baby's temperature is back to normal. He's still coughing, though. I ask the mother to bring her son to the clinic first thing in the morning and not to hesitate to call again if things worsen.

When I get off, the coons trill. Luke says, "I still have that headache."

"Do you?" I ask.

He looks straight at me. "I do," he says. "I have the worst headache I've had in my whole life."

I touch his arm. Luke's idea is that I should be able to fix what's wrong. I say, "Can I get you a Tylenol or something?"

"You could prescribe something stronger," Luke says. "Morphine."

The coons' masks shine.

"You want morphine?" I ask.

"I'm also catching a cold," he says.

"It's the weather," I say. "You just hate this heat."

I have the precipitous, dizzying feeling that I am not actually a part of this. I am not sitting on a Vancouver porch with my husband. His name isn't Luke. I even wonder if the coons in the yard are coons in love with a little girl named Holly. There seems to be something romantic in the air, but I don't know why.

I take Luke's hand. I say, "You won't always feel this rotten."

"I don't want anything from you. I know I said I want you to support me, but I was just mad."

"I'll give you money," I say.

"No," he says, "Seriously. I don't want it."

Together we tilt our heads to the sky, to the Big Dipper, and I think how the stars are way too high to reach. Even from the top of the peach tree, even on Luke's shoulders, I'd be way too short to touch a single one.

MARK ANTHONY JARMAN

Travels into Several Remote Nations of the World

Too great a hurry to discharge an obligation is a kind of ingratitude.
> – François, Duc de La Rochefoucauld (1613–1680)

Iam called south to the sunny counties just inches above Mexico's border where the fact of one's dying, that last exquisite border, is pushed straight down like a discreet sofa-bed, a quiet, expensive model that will never betray the fact that it has an ulterior motive, a hidden agenda, that it's guilty of being a sofa-bed.

At the Seattle airport the dedicated American customs man wonders, Why is your passport expired?

I was not expecting to travel.

And why is that?

My father just died. I'm on my way down to San Diego, to help my mother.

The customs man bows his head in regret, quickly waving me through. Perhaps he remembers his father dying in a distant city. The customs man's dark uniform adds weight to his empathy. I am now sanctioned, privileged, with special rights, special rites; I am the grieving son.

Was he a black man? Looking back, I think so. He wore gold glasses, took his duties seriously, as did my father. So early in the morning: and my memory is not reliable at that half-dark hour. The alarm rang at 4 a.m. and I leapt up like a scarecrow:

What!? What?! My primitive heart going like a gong. Then the knowledge seeping back. I have to crawl to the foggy airport. My father's heart squeezed shut. I imagine we have the exact model of heart, perhaps the same expiry date. A contest with my father then: I must live longer than he did. The big artery or vein on the left of the heart; widowmaker the doctors call it, as loggers term stray branches that weigh a ton and drop on your head from a world above.

Why does death involve so many airports, so many orange plastic seats? There was money to burn when Hot Wheels orange was cool, but then budgets got slashed and now we're stuck with that era's hue and cry.

Too many eras to kill, too many pasty pilgrims in my way, grim shuffling travellers who could have died easily before my father had to die. Like Hamlet, I want revenge. That gnarled codger by the orange seats. Why aren't you dead? I feel like grabbing his lapels, letting him know he should have keeled over first (a rat has breath). My father would be *mortified*. He was never one to make waves, to complain. I, for some reason, thrive on a diet of complaint, waves, a chameleon eating empty promises. I have inherited my father's English restraint and my Irish mother's craving for strife. Cold toast and warm beer and I'm stuck in the middle of them.

Plunging sideways down into San Diego the tiny plane tilts gleefully through dazzling whiter-than-white clouds. It's a riot. I love flying, love travelling. We wear green earplugs the size of bullets; the pilot stands our plane on one wing and we gaze straight down at the sunlit ocean peacock blue against the arid waste hills just north of Mexico. How many pilgrims are sneaking through the wired arroyos, sneaking through the gaps in the clouds, thinking now their life will begin? My parents go south every winter; these ones on the ground flood north, wily coyotes leading nervous chickens for a steep price.

Good luck, I wish them. Don't be careful, as they say. The brilliant round clouds we slice through – white floors and walls and shifting beckoning halls with muscular curves and sunlit arches – heavenly. I feel I could step out of the narrow plane and look for Dad.

No luggage to claim; I'll buy cheap shirts in Encinitas or wear my father's clothes, his baggy white dress shirts. I move away quickly from the propellers, look for the retired man from New Jersey in the Greek fisherman's cap who is to meet me at the bottom of the airport escalator. I'm glad my mother has suntanned friends here to help her.

How is she? I ask.

She's doing all right, he says. She's tough Irish, he says.

He is a serious man who limps from a wound received in the Pacific in WWII. The Japanese. My father and this man share an unspoken enemy.

We nose toward the palm-lined freeway. In a large gold car with Republican bumper stickers we converse about the state of the States. This man will go to the wall for you if you're on his side. I'm not sure if I'm on his side. Why is that? He seems so American, yet I cannot define why. He limps, but I would bet anything that he beats all comers at golf, tennis, or sack races. I sense WWII and the military have shaped him. He would believe roast beef at a table deserves a serious expression, not tomfoolery.

I'm almost forty with grey in my beard, but I still employ a voice for "adults," especially for friends of the parents.

Is this man relieved that it's my father and not him closed up in that silent drawer at the San Diego coroner's? I don't know. The drawers are kept cold and they shut on soundless rubber rollers.

As the man steers the golden car he tells me how much they liked my father in their close-knit complex above the beach. He says kind things about my father, recounts their shock, their sorrow.

Your father was a real gentleman, he says.

Suddenly this ranking seems the result of some obscure contest.

Thank you, I say, unsure of responses.

The kind man from New Jersey drives us north to the condos. I'm on I-5 yet again. The Canadian border to Mexico; I've driven every inch, every klick of the postwar infrastructure. Diamond lanes, trembling bridges, backdoor exits.

All the white shoes. Money made off the snowbirds when they're alive and money made off them when they're dead. How many Canadian tourists die down here every winter? All the dead souls in limbo, like their white shoes going to Goodwill. Don't tread on me.

I'm not going to blame the stars or the era, I'm going to blame the state everyone loves to hate; I want to join the rumble, put the boots to it, aim for the temple, the kidney, the midsection. California is verdant, exotic, lush, but each time I parachute in it seems more screwed up.

I love California, but I'm going to pretend to be Puritan for a minute. I'm going to hint at my superior morality.

I move up and down the coast in my father's blue rental car, cruising 101 up to the distant mortuary for paperwork or cheques, taking the old highway instead of the faster freeway and guiltily admiring beach towns and bent surf, casting my eyes over white walls of surf and soup, porpoises and unlikely-looking brown pelicans.

An offshore breeze, I think, should be good winter surfing.

My eye is happy when it should be grieving. Your father lost a father, etc. I flash up and down the coast, I drink of the holy water, I drink something dark on tap, and at night I squint at the security lights walking the ocean. Purple City. Sandpipers run back and forth in the waves, shorebirds like tiny light bulbs on claws.

California draws me in despite my misgivings. Whole populations ignoring the obvious. You have to admire them in a way. They're too close to it; they ditched their ID so long ago. You need to go away, but even when Californians travel they don't really go away from California. Not until much, *much* later.

California, once ahead of the curve, is now behind the curve, the curve is now up its ass. They pretend the curve is not up their ass; they pretend it's business as usual in a blind thrashing temple, a melancholy mosh pit with minor earthquakes doing the twist with the off-ramp.

A ghostly Mormon temple rises beside the perfect shrunken lanes of I-5. You are entering Mammon city limits in overdrive. The Japscrap car in front of me blows its sunroof and I'm covered in broken glass at 70 mph. Our hearts, our parts move, our broken parts conspiring to kill us or define us, black and white faces thrown through life like dice.

For an hour my father's clenched heart was a mad, glad god, a fist, and my father's thriving perfect brain had no more power, no clout; the arrogant brain received its comeuppance. The files helpless, staying there vibrating for agonizing minutes, still alive, hanging on, then particles wiped. Book and volume. In Africa they say when an elder dies a library burns down. I believe that is what they say.

In Solana Beach my mother and my cousin Pat feed me full of heaps of bacon and eggs and steaks, trying to use up groceries before we leave, trying to take care of me, trying to kill me.

In Solana Beach and Encinitas and Leucadia and Cardiff store-fronts are empty: blank computer shops and hardware stores with FOR LEASE signs; nailed-up boutiques and favoured bars run high and dry. This is their afterlife. A real-estate crash in the cosy beach towns of the North County and far worse in the less posh inland valleys, FOR SALE signs in every block, trash and tracts blowing at your feet, and lines of men gathered from all over Central America just to stand across from this shopping complex, to gather at the dry river. Time out of joint, failure in a sunny land with no tolerance for failure, no visible mythology of failure, only of sun, youth, cheesy surf guitars, wild success.

Here my father failed to live. My mother and I had to leave the husk of my father's body with strangers, with people we really disliked; we had to abandon him to the hands of Deck the cracker mortuary guy up in Oceanside, to Deck and his pimply crew. My mother and I failed.

What kind of name is Deck? Deck is riding a growth industry, riding a wave like a surfer. We're his cash cow. Deck the cracker is hiring trainees and selling death like a muffler warranty, like daffodils or crocuses. And there is no choice.

My mother is, what, seventy-seven, and she has to pay some smarmy stranger big bucks to burn her husband of forty-nine years; and she's told there's a lineup. My parents are Catholic, but they discussed it earlier and both decided on cremation, despite what their church says. Now it turns out everyone these days in southern California is dying; turns out it's the new thing, and everyone else discussed it earlier and wants to be burned, but there is a catch. There are only four crematoriums. No one's built a better mousetrap, or there is some serious denial.

It's not like I can say, Well, Deck, I guess we'll just take care of it at home, throw Dad on the barbie or a pyre of tires. We're not what you term "handy." I am sorry my father's snowbird death so inconvenienced the state and populace. There's a lineup. Totally. I mean like you can't just die without a little consideration. You need reservations to die, you need clout to get a decent table.

Maybe I can narrow (or broaden) my hatred to Oceanside. To the jacked-up cars with loud bass and the jacked-down cars with loud bass, looped lowriders, jarhead military haircuts, ugly post-modern avenues and cinderblock 7-Elevens, tiny tattoo shops, murals, moron pugilists, brown pelicans, tattered cabbage palms, brainwashed Chelseas and Dylans and Dees and Taras grunting and sweating in the paralytic traffic, pachucos and gangstas and rastas and deadheads and skaters and the booming bass I can hear loud and clear right inside the busy funeral home while waiting with my mother for Deck to receive us, to get to us, while waiting in the waiting room.

You can tell that the mortuary had once been a handsome Spanish design with a verdant courtyard of foliage but they've grafted some gruesome modern addition over the front. They've wrecked it, made it an easy metaphor, hidden the garden, the dark oak doors. Blinding aluminum doors now like a welfare office.

Aloo-minnie-um, my father would say, the English pronunciation of aluminum. Deck says, "Cree-mate."

I hope you never have to wait here with your mother and your dead father.

My brother-in-law worked in Oceanside as an engineer, but the office was fire-bombed and burnt during the L.A. riots. He lost his job. The riots are a very fresh memory here. The happy citizenry and the crawling truck driver at the wrong intersection taking the bricks to the head in the warm California sun. I was glancing at Shakespeare, Falstaff, with the TV on. I thought I watched the man die, live via a TV helicopter. It's a good design but how many objects can a skull take? I couldn't believe it when I read later he survived that particular welcome wagon. With some help he escaped them, escaped Deck.

My brother-in-law brags, I drove along the freeway beside Janet Jackson's limo.

Is that so, I say.

Perhaps I don't look suitably impressed because he asks, Do you even know who Janet Jackson is up in Canada? I don't say how I wish we didn't know, wish Canada wasn't swamped in American dreck.

The brother-in-law stops talking with his two sisters; disagreements over the dispersal of their mother's estate. The brother phones everyone to yell as if he is the new grouchy parent: Why wasn't his wife the real-estate agent! You all conspired against me! It's a plot!

To those with the hip-hop metal bass cranked up outside the funeral home: I hope for cancer of the testicles for you.

I wonder if an irrational hatred of Oceanside is part of the grieving process. I wonder if nostalgia can be exactly as bad as cancer or nitrates. Can we blame the platters of bacon and eggs Dad fried and ate every Sunday? My mother also had them and she's alive. I ate them too, ate them gladly. My father died the year of their fiftieth wedding anniversary. Just a few months short of half a century. We were going to throw a family party, get together and argue joyously. Instead a sedate funeral without a body.

My parents had never seen Italy, but finally made it there in what turned out to be my father's last summer. They didn't know it was the last time. They waited a long time for their tour. They were not ashamed to be tourists, to tour. Florence, Venice, Rome, Paris, London, Dublin, Galway, the Aran Islands. I doubt very much whether their thoughts drifted nine time zones west to an ugly stucco mortuary in Oceanside with a loud bass waiting curbside just for them.

A New England writer I admire grew to love Italy in the 1950s, the city velocity, country matters, dark-haired women and hunchbacked churches and familial servants. My parents never had servants. The writer's father died in a rooming house alone, as did his older brother, and the New England writer worried the same fate would befall him. He did not want to die alone, to have them find you quite a bit later up there with your hot plate and chipped green mug and can of chowder. He did not want to be like his father.

My father took his world tour just in time; my parents trod the fertile green earth, then the world yanked the carpet out from under their feet, the fecund black earth trod on them a little.

But my father came to what is considered a fast death, appearing to be healthier and happier than anyone else until that last hour or two; my father eluded the ruffian on the stair, as Houseman put it. The stairs, the sun, the sidewalks, gates, doors, crawling to the couch, my mother finding him later, the young doctor from the swimming pool working him over, serious but certain they'd found him in time, the ambulance looking for him in the heaped boxes of condos, and then the doctors at Scripps losing him after he arrived, after he finally seemed safe, to have found sanctuary: it probably did not feel a fast death that sunny morning, that afternoon (that sleeps so peacefully).

You were lucky, people say to me, believe it. You were very lucky not to see your father reduced to a shadow in a hospital bed, to a gowned skeleton with a hand you hold to yours. Far from the pelicans and porpoises in the breaking surf.

I should be grateful for something, but my brain feels like adjunctive pieces of lettuce and Velcro, like sodden newsprint.

When I married eons ago in Seattle, I borrowed a Sears suit. Now I stand at my father's funeral service in a borrowed Hugo blazer. Before I die I'll try to arrange for a jacket of my own. The faux gold buttons and dark blue-black cloth of the Hugo blazer make me realize: The Royal Navy doesn't know another class of '39 Petty Officer is gone. They may be tiring of such news. The World War II alumni must be dropping like flies now, fifty years after the event.

I wonder how his sister in England is taking the news (I read the news today, oh boy). My father's twin brother died during the war, died of pneumonia in a barracks. There are no other siblings, no parents left. When I spent time in London my relatives all remarked on how similar I was to my father; strangely, no one had ever said this to me in Canada. My father, it sometimes seems, has no people in Alberta. His people are back in the old country, or lost in the war, or they are snowbirds in flight, killing the winter somewhere warmer, Albertans fleeing to Victoria, Solana Beach, Phoenix, Mesa, Hawaii, even Fiji or Majorca or a sharp Greek rock in the sun.

They're retired from the clinic; everyone who knew my father is scattered or already dead.

Oxford is dead. The brick house at the corner of Banbury Road is dead. Twin brothers and a sister riding rickety English bicycles out into the English countryside with their despot father the painter: that life is gone, dead. Did it exist? The Trout pub. Narrow boats on the narrow river. The Great Depression. The Thermos of tea and oil paints and English landscapes (my father named after Frederick Leighton, the English artist). One of my grandfather's watercolours hangs now over my imitation rolltop desk, a used oak desk purchased when I was eighteen and working at my first job, trying to take on traditions. I never thought to ask my father what his twin brother was like.

My mother and father shed tradition like a snakeskin, bought clean modern furniture, shed the old country, never talking about England once they left. Seasick all the way on the boat and then a claustrophobic train, with three children, from Quebec to Edmonton, then staying with another family until they found a tiny house to rent. Never complaining about the winters at forty below zero or the watery tins of frugal Woodward's marmalade or the huge strange cavernous taverns or the locals who called him by the wrong name from day one. Leighton (William Leighton) did not correct them, amiably taking on his new identity, the new name Bill, along with the new country full of Bills. Leighton Jarman became Bill Jarman, in a thrice. I admire this calm chameleon adaptability. I don't know if I ever heard him complain about anything. Where did I pick up my tendency from? My Irish mother? My father's father?

Granny travelled out to the new world for a visit, to see the growing tribe of Canucks and perhaps to get away from "the old boy" in Oxford. She looked around the treeless postwar suburb and declared that my parents had done the right thing after all. They could not have had this many kids in crippled postwar England. In this way Hitler has something to do with my existence in Canada. Granny knitted me a Rupert the bear in a tiny red sweater with speckled buttons (I stared into the depths of those beautiful buttons), made us special tea, returned to England, and later had a mild stroke. A shutter coming down, my aunt told me. Granny travelled back in time. Her first words after the stroke: "Kay's pregnant again," referring to my mother's seemingly endless condition. My Granny is the only grandparent I remember. The nice one, it is implied by my mother.

Bill did not return for Leighton's father's funeral. My father's father who forbade him to leave England, who was a physiotherapist and made my father become a physio. My father's father who referred no patients to him, then at the last minute promised the entire practice, after the transatlantic tickets were already paid for, if my father would stay in England.

My father was prepared to throw in the towel, but my Irish uncle forced my parents to the boat. My father's father played violin and painted; he was feared and he looked down on my Irish mother. I wish I knew the whole gang better. I suspect my brothers and I are more like the old boy, the grandfather, or like the Irish faction, than we are like Dad. My younger brother has Grandpa's nose and plays the violin, plays any instrument. All of us love to complain and to change our minds at the last minute.

My father left his father's body there as I wordlessly leave my father in another country, a foreign country.

I love the Great Plains but haven't lived here in the ice and windchill for a decade. I was an émigré wimp sneaking out to the balmy coast when the coast was still cheap. Travel back for a father's funeral and a childhood city seems charged with significance, symbolism, melancholy. Will this new world become my old country? The one I never mention?

I stroll past the bungalow I lived in for decades. Perched on a ravine's edge, this bungalow is what I think of as the family home. After twenty years my parents' children grew up and drifted away, voting with their feet, and so my mother and father sold the bungalow, moving to a high-rise closer to the river. Luckily they sold the house before the oil boom crashed and before we kids could move back in. New owners dropped in buckets of cash, chopped open the blond bricks, went up into the air to add a storey, another layer on the cake. Did they find what they were looking for? Did they find our tortoise that took to the subfloor and never came back from its exile in the underworld? I dwell on the towering elms and blond bricks; dwell on the series of wars and bombs and parties and passports and ocean liners and trains and bicycles and moving vans and houses that led me to this roseate house on the ravine that rolls slowly down to the North Saskatchewan river, and then just as neatly led me away again.

As children we drank out of this dirty river when thirsty, played war games in the eroded cliffs and coulees, watched a ten-year-old friend slip suddenly through the ice and drown in the speeding muddy river underneath. Two seconds and he was gone under a ceiling of ice, never seen by us again, ending up two provinces over. His family was large and poor; I'm ashamed to admit his drowning didn't make a huge impression on me. It didn't seem a clear lesson. Death always visits someone else; the drowning boy proved that nicely. Thus I would never die, and no one in *my* family would ever die.

Every winter we crossed the frozen river in our polished HBC mukluks, crossed broken ice floes to see the other side, despite our parents' desperate orders, their unwavering warnings. A kid doesn't know what a parent feels and vice versa: we couldn't see the other side and we had to see the other side.

Don't go near the river. Did we listen? We went straight to the river. We took to the river. Take me to the river. The Ukrainian mayor was corrupt. He was kicked out of office and voted back in and kicked out again. He put in a modern bridge but the river pushed it over, made its comment on his regime.

I was young and judgemental, hated the mayor. Now I'm old and judgemental and I hate the memory of that mayor.

February in my childhood city is dead as a snakeskin, and some familiar streets are more depressing than I can under-stand. I never found them depressing before. I feel I no longer belong. I tell myself they are just streets, simply blocks I knew where I raked my parents' leaves, met the young woman walking her dog, and was beaten up by Protestants. A suicide lived there behind laurel and fragrant lilac, a Bishop the women liked here on the crescent skirting the ravine, a high-school girlfriend over there, someone's older brother was committed to an asylum from that house.

I begin to worry that this fresh old life has the power to drag down my tired new life; an old sunny life is still here and not here, in the back of your head like a brother you don't see, a father you don't know.

I was born here when the oil boom was born. I'm hovering in the air but no one knows me. I left this city to go to the lake and swim in the weeds, to go to Newfoundland or Seattle, to go to Montana or Iowa, to go to Ireland or Madrid. Now that I'm back in Edmonton I wish to walk miles, refusing offers of rides in the cold weather. I walk and I can't talk. I want air, want my legs working after the flights, airports and meals and pews and drinks; I want to slip again on my dear dirty snowbanks. No one there. That life is gone. It's no longer home. But it is what used to be home, it's still what *was* home.

At the Cathedral Basilica where Wayne Gretzky married a pregnant starlet the priest compares my father to a saint, but I find myself counting the empty pews. Is this a saint's reward? Too many of my parents' friends are dead; numerous friends are out of the country; many haven't heard the news yet. Do the dead ones hear the news first? He was a saint but still, is this what a good life comes to? The church seems half empty. I resolve to be more evil. My father died at seventy-three. I'll probably die at seventy-three no matter what I do, whether I'm a jerk or not. I'm going to drink more Big Rock and drive faster, ignore cholesterol, scarf more cheddar-flavoured corn curls, club harp seals, badmouth Peter Pocklington at every opportunity. I know this is not a lesson my father would approve of.

My father's church has high empty air between stones with a greenish cast, flawless white grout, echoing tile floors, and shining oak pews that breathe oil and incense, the same polished arches and acres of oak where I genuflected as an altar boy decades ago, rising before dawn to catch the sparking trolley on 102nd Avenue.

Black primeval winter mornings I saw sparks jumping ten blocks away, a cream-coloured art deco trolley drawing toward me, toward the bus-stop bench, blue sparks opening from the frozen wires in front of Elaine Prodor's house (she would marry my best friend), blue sparks by Mike Starko's house (my mad scientist friend). It was so dark out at 6:30 a.m. It would never be light again. I hopped up and down on the icy walk, grunting in the cold, too cold for the bench, trying to keep blood moving. I think the trolley cost fifteen cents. I was a child, bundled up and riding a trolley to this massive cathedral my Dad helped build overtop the original church. My father gave epistles from the same lectern where I speak for his funeral. I remember Dad speeding here every Sunday morning in his dark green Oldsmobile, dragging his barbarian kids out of bed, fighting with us and hitting the gas, fighting with his four sons and two daughters every Sunday morning, battling over going to this stupid church, as I called it. Cursing his religion and church.

Still he seemed happy with his faith. And now that I'm back inside the Cathedral for my father's funeral I find I actually approve of the idea of a temporal or physical base, like the Mormon monstrosity beside Interstate 5, a whited sepulchre, some impressive, terribly costly temple where you can be baptized and bored to tears and lectured and harried and married and buried. In a way it glues a life together, offers to anchor it. I have no such anchor now.

Where will I be buried? My spirit will drift like a radio station fading away into North Dakota or the Queen Charlotte Islands.

The 7-Eleven near my house on the west coast has recently added a bank machine and a mini post office, but they don't seem to offer the Cathedral's kind of cradle-to-grave services. At 7-Eleven there are no confessionals, no relics under the altar, no tombs, no votive candles with a coin box. The 7-Eleven does sell loaves and fishes, but there are no German stained-glass windows showing the Stations of the Cross. And there are no pews of sad striking women.

A high-school sweetheart sits primly in the oak pews at my

father's funeral. I'm glad she came; I was once closer to her than anyone I knew. My sweetheart and I necked down the ravine, necked by the museum, necked by the river (*les lieux de memoire*, sites of memory). I remember my teenage hand pulled to the source of life in the pines behind her parents' huge house. She had athletic energy, appetite, a winning smile and large brown eyes. We had everything, we were doomed. I let her down and she let me down. She made me nervous, bumbling. I was naïve, hopeless. It took years but we found other lives to inhabit, other humans to follow.

A general had once lived in her family's huge house on the avenue and her brothers found a WWII pistol hidden in the attic.

I remember furious times with this girlfriend, fits of jealousy at drunken parties, stomping out to whatever wrecked car I owned with no fender or no first gear or no reverse and driving madly over the bridges crossing ravines, driving west toward the Rocky Mountains on three cylinders, my girlfriend calling, chasing me out the door a fraction of a second too late, hesitating on the lawn, then returning to her inebriated critical friends. It must have looked good to someone watching: a porch light and adolescent melodrama, a Hopper painting jumping to life.

A hundred miles later on the Yellowhead highway, halfway to the beautiful Rockies, I'd run out of gas, turn off the radio, steer the silent car over to the shoulder, walk across the highway and thumb back to the city, covering the same ground over and over. She waited once at my house to see if I was all right. We made up again, said how much we loved each other again. We did love each other but I think we were wrong, not meant for each other, and that's a hard thing to know at the moment, when you've staked what seems like everything on being right, when you think she must be the one. It feels like having an arm sawn off but it's not. I worried about losing her but never once thought about losing a parent; at that age you would probably welcome the idea.

There were about a dozen kids in my girlfriend's family. Her mother liked to fly down to Las Vegas and gamble, and she liked a drink once in a while. She died too young and I didn't make the funeral, was in the States. Looking for her youngest kid the mother would say: where is that little mistake? The mother wore big mumus. I'd tell her how good she looked and I meant it in a way. I wasn't attempting to be Eddie Haskell. My girlfriend's mother liked me and I liked her mother. We flirted. Funny how often I grew to like the mother better than the daughter.

Friday nights my girlfriend and I and our friends drained cases of Molson Golden and listened to Dan Hicks & His Hot Licks wail on my Baycrest stereo. We drank a lot in that house I rented after high school, breaking doors and coffee tables and burning couches and curtains. I was eighteen. She had to be home at midnight. The band sang: *I scare myself, just thinking about you*. We were late. I'd rush her back to her house, to the gate, have to touch her again before she went back to her mother.

I study the serious faces in the echoing pristine Cathedral. No one else at the funeral seems to be daydreaming of clumsy adolescent trysts. No one else is thinking of sex. Am I sick, or is this one of those situations no one admits to?

Everyone is invited to a reception in the church basement, but she doesn't descend the terrazzo stairs, doesn't show. Maybe she's on a break from work. Maybe she wants to avoid me, our long non-history. We had a protracted painful breakup. I will call her, I think, thank her for coming, thank her for the card she sent to my mother, but I fail to pick up my mother's phone.

Another woman attends my father's funeral. It takes me a minute to realize who she is. She used to play with my younger sister. She was a freckled and funny kid. Then a fast few years later I was swimming and saw her standing on a raft, saw her dripping water and grown up, a tall university student. The silver lake held us and an overcast sky; cool air and wet spare swimsuits and no one around. Her skin still fair and freckled, eyes dark, her face serious, pushing her hair back and talking to me about her brothers and her classes. No one else seemed to be around: no fibreglass boats, no noise, no engines, no smiling parents, just two of us, raft tilting with silky waves and weeds and our feet and hands, two bodies in a freezing lake with young skin and hair and big American cars that ran well, with time on our hands and matters weighing on our mind. Isn't that why you go back alone to the childhood cabin on the lake? To swim far past the raft or row a leaky skiff into the reeds, acquire a little distance, perspective, think things over? To think about that other fated person in the city?

We talked at the raft but I never said: Would you like to go out with me? That tack seemed too obvious, too awkward. We had a history and we didn't have a history. Her light hair had the faintest tinge of red. (Is that what is meant by strawberry blonde?) I was melancholy over something, someone, possibly the loss of my high-school girlfriend years before, or the loss of someone more recent, or maybe just the marble clouds moving over the lake. I like to dwell on things for a time, get my money's worth.

I felt old. I might have been twenty-two. I thought I was far too old for her: two or three years between us. Events in my life made me feel like a loser, like Prufrock. While the priest reminisces about my father I dwell on *carpe diem* for a moment, extract my money's worth out of that one. I love to torture loss, squeeze it like a free packet of shampoo.

My father used to swim across to the other side of Wizard Lake, turn in the lily pads, and swim home. Perhaps he needed to get away from his six savage kids. As a child I never considered that. I did worry a speedboat would not see him, would run its propeller over his broad back. He worried I'd drown in the North Saskatchewan River. Or did he worry? I was hitchhiking once and he drove right past me in his dark green Oldsmobile. It was pretty hands-off parenting for him.

I knew my athletic high-school girlfriend all too well. I never knew the freckled woman at the lake. And who comes down the measured church stairs to the basement reception? She is charming, smiling easily; she seems excited by the event. It is good to see her, to talk with her. She's funny, bright, she's alive. She is not dead, not yet. She laughs with my brothers and sisters. I believe she married and divorced a doctor. Her father was a doctor and a gentleman farmer, and their family was well off. They had land and cattle, a front-end loader, a speedboat, a perfect pier. Our weary pier was always falling over. I think about her years ago in that tiny swimsuit that should not have been a shock but still was a shock, the little sister all grown up, a college woman, an attractive archetype shivering in front of me and now in a Cathedral in February I feel guilty. I'm forgetting something; I forget what I'm forgetting.

I'm forgetting that my father is not at the funeral. He's still in a lineup of the dead turistas in California. He is with Deck. I left my father with strangers. His ashes will fly up later in the week. People on the plane won't know he's there under their heels. We ignore the dead.

My sister feels I should have somehow carried his tall body to the front of the line, past those other newly dead waiting to be burned, should have walked his body over the mountains or burnt his body myself, carried his ashes home cupped in my hand. My sister hints that it's ridiculous to have a memorial service for our father when he's not even here. Maimed rites.

My sister is right. I should have done more, but my mother and I did what we could dealing with the coroner and arguing with the assholes in the funeral "home," and we hugged the tearful Jewish neighbours who had helped Mom, who embraced us and cried, men and women all crying ("The Jewish are like that," my mother informs me). We said goodbye to the lovely grimacing snowbirds gathered here from all over the continent and we gave away Mom and Dad's new groceries and filled out forms and wrote cheques and packed up and returned the rental car and then we flew home on a milk run through five cities.

My peaceful father was beyond our help. I had flown to California to help my mother. My mother and I made our decisions, made our peace or failed to make our peace, then we cleared out, made our milk run, unsaid words in our mouths, a taste of ashes in our mouths.

Before we fled California I phoned Sharon long distance: "When I die don't give me to Deck. Don't let Deck get his hands on me. If I die push me over a cliff, shove me off Ten Mile Point in a burning boat." She doesn't know what I'm going on about.

In grocery stores I am irritated when people push up closer and closer, bump me, as if this will magically alter the speed of the checkout line. My mother does exactly this at the airport, kicking her luggage inches ahead when the line hasn't moved,

edging ever closer to the travellers ahead of her, nervously shifting her weight from foot to foot and moving closer. She also sur-
prises me with a huge tip to the man who guides us about three
feet from the curb to the lineup inside the glass doors. We're
early so my mother and I luck into a special flight carrying three
pilots from San Diego to L.A. We all put our earplugs in to dull
the small plane's engine noise. Every one of the pilots has
perfect hair and aviator sunglasses. They hoist a bag and smile
on the sunny, eye-piercing tarmac. They've bought into the
image, model it for us like a Sears ad.

In the airport in Utah my mother, never good with directions,
walks through the wrong door, one that would lead her right back
to LAX, back to her husband. Dad always knew the way so my
mother didn't have to. I catch up and take her arm. In Utah the
winter light is like purple flowers, like lavender. I like Utah for
some reason. There is ice on the wings, snow on the ground. It
feels scary and real and alive.

Deck is seeing some Okie couple while my mother and I wait to
see Deck, eavesdropping. Perhaps it's an Okie mother and son.
Would it cost less if we didn't have the graveside service? the
Okies ask.

Deck replies in his smooth southern accent, his voice almost
whispering, almost breaking: Why, then he'll be aaalllll alone.

Okay, they say, we'll pay for that, I guess.

After the winter flights and cut flowers and the service and
receptions and cheese and finger sandwiches, after this my
mother and father's children get together and laugh; we can't
stop laughing. It's 2 a.m. My mother and my brothers and sisters
at the family dining-room table now perched twenty storeys up
over the frozen North Saskatchewan River where the small boy
went under the ice so many years before. At this old oblong table
laughing is easy – gallows humour and worn family jokes that
surprisingly make my mother happy.

Glad someone can laugh, she says to us, and this is sweet
relief, to not be causing trouble, to have her want to hear our
laughter. She quotes her mother: "God is good – and the divvil's
not such a bad fellow either."

Tough Irish, said the man from New Jersey.

Mom wants us to help ourselves to Dad's clothes.

This tweed jacket would look nice on you, she says.

O.K. I put my arm into the sleeve of his tweed jacket and a wasp stings me. In the middle of winter. It's like a fast hammer blow. I jump, as I did with the alarm clock blaring at 4 a.m.

Maybe Dad doesn't want me to wear his jacket.

Nonsense, my mother says. He wouldn't do something like that. Would you like his bathrobe?

No thanks. I take things I don't want as souvenirs, to appease my mother and to remind me of my father. I wear my dead father's shirts, carry away two understated ties.

Waxwings struggle to stay alive in the mountain ash trees; they get drunk on the fermented mountain ash berries; and the curving snowy river valley seems so cold, so frozen. I'm a wimp now, used to the moderate west coast now, the lack of extremes. What can live here at forty below? I did, over half of my life. I like it here. Extremes can be better.

So many of the old people have fled one way or another, exile or death or amnesia (a special ambrosia?). Perhaps it's better to not know, better to hear the news too late, to not attend, to be otherwise engaged on a white shore, a white hotel in the tropic of cancer, a charming landscape not too far from an invisible airport.

If you don't know, you don't have to go to the airport and wait in line, don't have to know. Death may not get tired but we do.

Deck works over the poor Okies:

Son, your father is mighty proud of you right this minute up in heaven. Some people come in here asking for cardboard coffins. Work hard all your life and what will your family give in return? Gold? Silver? Oak? Velvet? Scenes of the Last Supper etched on the handles? No. They want cardboard.

Now you can just imagine what transpires fairly quickly when you set that cardboard and the defenceless body of your loved one straight down into the cold, cold, wet ground.

My father was a director, and his father a director, and I followed them into this calling. I never imagined I'd hear families yammering for cardboard. They say you got to change with the times but maybe some American families still feel a little concern, a little tug at the heart.

Now your basic bronze-lined concrete vault keeps at bay certain predictable graveside elements, say your basic air, water, insects, tree roots, rodents, vermin. Prettiest little vault set right into a nice hillside.

Vermin?! Oh oh oh . . .

Now Mama, it's all right, it'll be all right. There there.

There is silence. My mother and I grimace in the waiting room.

A vault you say? says the son.

A bronze-lined, concrete, secure, protected hillside vault. Beautiful site.

Like one of them fay-roes in Egypt?

No one really knows my father. No one really knows his son. People see me in front of them but I'm a cartoon character really.

They know that exactly nine months after my father's funeral we have a new baby boy. Like all our other sons, our baby's big Winston Churchill head is stuck between my wife's legs, and so out come the scalpels. My son comes in past the blades screaming and my wife almost dies from blood loss. All because of me and my old man and his old man, etc. And because of Hitler.

I hold the newest baby in my arms for its first few hours, soothing my son with the tip of my little finger in his mouth like a nipple while waiting for news from the doctors or midwife. Sorry, little guy, I have no milk for you. They can't give our baby to my wife because they're trying to staunch the bleeding, trying to keep her alive, and it's taking a long time.

Sharon is cleaned up; she gets fluids, IV, they wipe all the blood away, and she looks like a truck hit her. Drained and at the same time swollen like a balloon. Our four-year-old says, Jeez, you look rotten. Sharon came very close to dying. They pumped in units of blood and oh the fingers were flying with tiny stitches on the womb walls and muscles that gave up when the child was pulled away.

The baby was holding her together. Then the baby went out into the world of lights. I had a green mask on. They stitched and stitched. In the middle of this bloody mayhem the old-school Oriental surgeon leaned his small spectacled face over her and said, Mrs. McCartney! You must never have another baby! Another baby will kill you!

Death death death death. After my wife like a bird-dog. Taking my father and my good friends. Levi and his brain tumour, Craig and insulin shock. Sharon's mother, Sharon's sister, every one of my mother's friends, the fireman down the street with three young daughters the same age as our sons, and Barbara the elderly neighbour: we went in on fixing the fence between us. She died and we didn't know for weeks. Her TV got louder and louder over the new fence, and then the TV stopped and she was gone.

Doesn't death ever get tired? Downsize? Hire a consultant? Does it do time-and-motion studies? Want a career change? Does it, like me, have an unsettled feeling that things some-where else are livelier, want to check out things in Samarra?

My mother is pushing eighty and she seems lonelier every month, but she is still alive. I don't think she'd trade that, I don't think she'd take the alternative. Weekends are worst, she says. She has outlived her doctor and her husband and her friends, but she's alive: takes her walk every day, plays bridge, hits a golf ball, takes putting lessons, yoga lessons, attacks a crossword. When the traffic light says WALK she beats everyone across, as if it's a race, as if heavy money is riding. My sisters and I laugh at her frantic pace, wishing that energy had more outlets.

We all live in different cities, voting with our feet. We're grumpy but alive. Actually I feel more than alive. In fact, I'd go so far as to say, We're all right, Jack. Death makes me feel this way, makes me giddy, even about the food in the hospital base-ment when my newest child is born. The arrayed juices, hot cocoa or Earl Grey tea, bowls of fruit, hot rich gravy, and plump mountains of mashed potatoes: I've never tasted better than this. I'm serious. I actually vow to come back just for the food. The string of deaths has perversely had the effect of making me happier, easier to please.

Now every detail is rich, significant. I can juggle an orange and decide whether I catch it or not. In the parking lot I draw in real air. I can split wood and drive nails. I buy new books or hear new bands I know my dead friends would have loved. They'll never hear another thrilling note, and I can buy a new tape every day. I can rant stupid opinions, and then change my mind. My friends are dead and my father too, so now I appreciate every moth and spider and heal-all in the design.

Death has made me obnoxiously positive, positively obnoxious. I look into the sky and find blue shadows and blinding pyres of light. I can punch a wall, drive too fast leaving the hospital, and holler out a car window: I'm alive! I can be charming and I can be an asshole. The most mundane options intoxicate me. Because suddenly I know a dozen people who lost every single option.

When our beautiful babies are overdue, when they hesitate at the gate, folk wisdom maintains that lovemaking hastens the event. Some of the pregnant women are insatiable.

I wonder if it was the same for my father and mother. They would never dream of talking to us about such matters. (Did you think I meant country matters?) I contend death can take an exact cue from all of us, from this final frenzy of intimacy; death knows what it can do with itself. It can roughly do what we've been doing to ward it off.

I concede my cranky message is less than articulate or uplifting, but nonetheless, if you talk to the cracker undertaker down in California I want to be certain you pass it on. For to me the smallest detail is now rich and significant.

In the ravine behind our old house, birds keep saying whatever it is, riotous and dark against the white bark, stammering over and over in their bird boroughs, alive and drunk despite the odds of a northern winter.

I saw heartbreakingly perfect flowers at the Cathedral; flowers spread in Mom's white apartment twenty storeys above the frozen river. My father's coat stung me. Even in winter, earth a motor blowing wasps and blossoms.

BARBARA LAMBERT

Where the Bodies Are Kept

I don't have a lot I want to think about just now. The job is finished, the order has gone off by Federal Express, the house is silent as the grave. Truly, the phrase describes the state I fall into at those times when one thing is finished and I have no idea what the next thing is going to be, the break I've been longing for, for weeks. Without a moment for relaxation, decomposition begins.

So I turn my mind to Kate Rutherford instead. Thank god for neighbours, I say – thank god for Kate at least, pretty Kate – for her glorious imprudence, which I can take a good close look at when my own life does that trick of dissolving and filling up my lungs with dread. Kate lives just up the street on the edge of Lighthouse Park, in a noted West Vancouver house, five levels of glass and stone. It was about three years ago that she smashed her husband's BMW into a hydro pole with such force that, among other things, the whole neighbourhood had to do without power over the crucial dinner hour. How many candle-lit romances did she spark, I wonder – how many families talked and listened in the flickering strangeness of their sudden cave-like homes?

Some weeks later, Kate made it home from the hospital, in a taxi, alone.

I imagine how that was – how she stood in the hall of that great glass house where the inside merged with the outside, the dripping cedars all around, the glass roof streaming with rain. I picture her tugging at a strand of hair, pulling that curl until she could chew the end of it, tasting the familiar sliding crunch as the hair dampened and went limp between her teeth.

I listen – not to the rattle of a shingle on my own roof, but to how that house of Kate's must have echoed as she stood there in the hall.

She was staring at a tall Italian table that held a vase of flowers, five purple irises, a few narcissus, a large white lily – all a few days old. Beside the vase was a note, on a sheet from one of Charlie's prescription pads. "I've sent the children out to my sister in the Valley," she read, "until you decide to get your feet back on the ground. I won't be home for dinner by the way – late surgery."

No slam-bang arrival then, to wait for – three teenagers bursting in the door, dumping down their bags, carping at one another, scattering their coats and shoes: not embarrassed by her presence, no! Just glad, relieved, *obviously* glad to have her home.

I feel the closing-in, the chill: how that glass-roofed hallway shrank down to something smaller than a block of ice, how she hung suspended in the cube of silence, like a speck, *until you get your feet back on the ground*.

Dreamlike it would feel, to be so frozen – and then a sudden thaw, a rush of vindication, as she went over to the mirror, checked the face that had been miraculously spared, remembered how she'd trembled when she made it up an hour before, taking care to do it all the way he liked it: mascara but not eyeliner, shadow of the most delicate bruised blue.

She snatched her purse from the chair by the door and rifled through her wallet. It was too late for the bank. Anyway, Charlie had closed their joint account some time ago. Still, she had enough for a day or so. She could hear the taxi backing-and-filling down near the street, tearing up the pebbles, as if the driver had run into some sort of trouble in the dark and the rain. So she ran after him – slipping on the gravel, ripping her stocking, bloodying her knee, muddying her camel coat horribly. She hammered on the hood just as the car was creeping out into the road. As she settled into the back once more, she caught the driver's eye in the mirror. She saw the way he was reassessing her. She said to herself, Well, what do I care?

She tried to make him race along Marine Drive. The road twisted past houses like her own braced on the cliffside, also English-looking beamed and leaded manors, and the charming seaside cottages where bankers and stockbrokers had retired to grow roses and putter around. She hurried him across Lion's Gate Bridge, and through the darkening park, to Vancouver proper. "Take me to the West End," she told him, then. "Oh, I don't know – just anywhere."

All of this happened before I knew Kate of course, before I suffered the enormous change in my own life that caused me to move here, to this part of West Vancouver whimsically known as Tiddly Cove.

I bought a house at the crossroads of The Glen and The Glen. One of those streets is actually The Glen Wynde, but as everyone who needs to know this is presumed to know already, the signpost doesn't bother to explain. This struck me as a good-natured omen when I first viewed the house. You could hardly get lost, could you, if no matter which way you went you were still on the street that led you home?

Tiddly Cove. It is a metaphor of course, though the actual streets are right there on the map. It is the invention of cartoonists, who have made it the epitome of what eastern journalists like to refer to as Lotus Land. And why not? I said, the morning after I arrived. Let them call it anything they want, the poor buggers, still up to their ankles in snow. I jogged along The Glen, following glimpses of the sea. The air was full of robins, and the squeaks and peeps of a hundred other birds, the rush of wings. Bluebells bordered the road on one side, and red-leafed masses of false-geranium in tiny pinkish flower. On the other side I was passing a heavily wooded area, huge alders, the trunks spattered with a brilliant greenish crust of lichen. Then the woods gave way to the small harbour – a sailboat bobbing at its buoy, a beached canoe – and sunlight played upon the rocks, the driftwood, the water, and the scent of broom tangled up the air.

There was a grassy nubbled park a little further along the road – one remaining apple tree (that morning in full bloom) from what had once been a seaside orchard. The dewy meadow flashed with a scattering of small reflected fires. I sat on a rock, in the sun. Across the street, and all the way up the hill, the gabled, shingled houses peered through their pocketing of trees and shrubs and flowers. How could it be possible that anyone – *anyone* – (of course I was thinking of myself) could not be happy here?

I design fabric for a living – *surface decoration, a smoke-and-mirrors sort of thing*, the aunt who raised me used to say. That was back in the days when she still dreamed I might improve my looks, no matter what, and pick off a doctor or a lawyer. The way Kate Rutherford nailed Charlie, long before he even got to med school, would have struck Aunt Jackie as ideal.

Yes I deal entirely in surface. I would love to go deeper, believe me. I would love to illuminate the ticking of the clockwork of the universe, I would love to be able to make clear, in the curve of a woman's cheek, or the lines of a rock, or the whiteness of a flower, how everything relates to every other thing. Also I'd love to have an artist's verve, the audacity of Attila Lukacs, or Picasso, or the nerve to wrap the Reichstag, the confidence that rests on supreme technical control. But the fact is that I embarked on the creative life without a scrap of talent. I have the eye, and I have the horrid burning itch – also the bottomless pit that I sometimes think might be filled up by recognition – but I still can't draw a line.

Perhaps that's why I have always felt such a peculiar fellow-feeling for Kate Rutherford. Even the first time I met her I couldn't help a shiver of recognition. My moving truck had just driven away; I was surrounded by crates, upturned chairs, baskets crammed with earrings, socks, and undies, also all the paraphernalia of my craft, which I was going to have to fit into a house far more cramped and decrepit than I had fondly thought when I closed the deal. And now this woman was advancing through my gate. A little out of focus she seemed to me, but I was tired – a face that put me in mind of a shade plant, some determined wavering flower.

Yet there was something formidable here as well. That crisp white dress, those brown-and-white shoes with nail-hole patterning, that creamy English-looking skin against the sprightly blue-black curls. A well-kept woman in her forties. *Well kept.* I found myself pondering that phrase. She was starting up my stairs, frowning in a way that made me think I'd transgressed some quaint neighbourhood decree. She tut-tutted at the broken riser, lowered herself into the shredding wicker sofa the previous owner had left on my porch (was I catching whiffs of a fruity perfume, or was that brandy?), crossed her lovely legs, unaware that the tops of her knee-high nylons showed, and – turning on me violet eyes set oddly wide apart – said, in a tone of perfect ladyhood which all the same acknowledged how this was wonderfully absurd, "I thought perhaps you'd like to pour me a cup of tea."

Later, of course, various neighbours told me all about the leap to freedom she had taken, a year or so before.

Kate kept the taxi driver cruising up and down the West End streets. It was an adventure for him, she could see. "If you get me through this, I'll buy you a drink," she said, "except – oh shame! – come to think of it, I don't actually drink any more."

"No problem," he replied. Perhaps his religion did not permit him to drink, anyway. His dark silky eyes still studied her. His fine brown hands were lazy and adept on the wheel. He understood her kind exactly – *This rich woman,* his expression said, *one of those pretty bitches who pour on the charm if they don't know you, especially if they don't know you, as long as it stays that way* – and he knew full well that when she had found a place to spend the night he would not be invited in: she would not unwind his turban, all those yards of crinkled folds; she would not wrap it around and around her and do a dance for him; and he (appalled, intrigued, against his will), well, he would not *be* there, that was all – for even in imagination she got stymied. A silly phrase came into her head, and tears came to her eyes. *"We're going to have to liberate that naughty girl in you."* That was Fred, the therapist. A lovely man, the one bright light of her hospital stay, the way he had sat and looked at her, with his bulging beautiful green eyes.

The West End, where tall buildings shouldered one another, filled with cubicles of light, filled with breath and life and anonymity. At last Kate saw a promising for-rent sign – an old house jammed tight among the high-rises – a third-floor walk-up, a one-room studio. The driver turned off the meter while she settled the details of the rent, while she wrote out a cheque that would bounce, but she'd deal with that when she had to. The driver's name was Sanjit, and he did not think that she should leave her husband. He said *for gratis*, as he put it, he would drive her home right now. All the same, he took her over to Canadian Tire so she could buy a cheap electric kettle, and a mug, and a roll of foam. "Though I certainly intend to have a proper bed," she told him as he helped her up with the awkward roll – "but the foam will be useful when the children want to have friends sleep over, don't you think?"

"You intend to bring your little children here?"

"They're not so little. But yes, of course."

He gave her his card. "Better tonight you think it over. Any time you call, I'll take you home."

She made a list in her head, that first night, as she tossed and turned. Ikea, yes. She'd make do with the simplest things, for a while. She charted a course for the next day – Duthie's, Ikea, Safeway – the necessary triangle of books and furnishings and food. She pictured this from every angle (a geometric figure that always skirted the liquor store), set it upright, laid planks of demanding simple work across the apex. She would give Charlie quite a surprise with the things that she might do.

Next morning she went through the ads. Home-Sewers Wanted was one she finally had to tick. But come along, Kate, she told herself – here you are, with the one chance of your life to do all the things you've always wanted to do. Last night you went on and on about how you used to have a way with words. Last night, as I recall, you were going to write a mystery.

All night, or so it seemed – flat on her back because of her ribs – she had watched a fan of light wavering across her ceiling, which brightened, dimmed, for no reason she could see. Shadows brushed across it, the branches of some sparse city tree. All night she had contained the fact of where she was within the skin of fantasy. She must have read a thousand mysteries these last few years while she waited for Charlie to come home, and hadn't she always said she could do better? Some people make good money doing that.

I can see her exactly, the way she sits up in bed when that thought comes to her. The bare floor, the single thermal blanket, the snippy up-tilt of her chin. "Well, Kate, you will jolly well write one too!" The tone of her father, the Brigadier-General, later an inspector of schools.

~

So now, on the day that this is really all about, Kate has been living in that apartment for a year and a month. She has not had a drink in that whole time. And when she looks back at the desert she has crossed, she wonders at the fact that she has made it. *"Be patient, Katie. You'll be a different person in a year."* The words of the lovely green-eyed Fred. After she left the hospital she saw him once a week for a while. He gave her courage for a while.

Today, though, she is impatient with herself. She is stepping off a bus at the corner of Hastings and Columbia, in the meanest section of the east end of town. She is facing an unaccustomed challenge, true, but this nervousness is quite absurd. She knows that her mother, had her mother been alive, would have told her to buck up. Of course, her mother would have told her, also, to get the hell out of there immediately and go home.

After she left Charlie she took on a job doing piecework sewing, for a jam factory on the edge of Chinatown, in an area of strip clubs and by-the-hour hotels. Her usual routine is to come across town by bus and pick up a week's worth of sewing and hurry straight home to the West End. She does the sewing in the small and dreadful hours, when in any case a deep ache keeps her sleepless. Her children are still out in the Valley. Charlie has threatened to get a restraining order if she takes the Greyhound out there again and tries to pick them up after school; and in fact they hardly want to see her anyway. They loved her all the time she was in trouble, but now that she has changed they allow themselves to feel the shame. Soon though – oh soon! – they will all be singing a different tune, Charlie too.

Normally, she would never have traipsed along this street. But today she is on a mission. The detective book, which she barely dared to dream of a year ago, has moved into the realm of hard research. Charlie would be amazed at how disciplined she has been. She has never once gone out in the morning, as she would have loved to, and walked down to Starbucks for a coffee, then on to English Bay. Instead she has sat herself firmly down at the kitchen table and filled pages and pages with notes and plans and sketches – and further notes: technical and scientific and forensic, garnered during long conversations on the phone – until this has come to be the actual total of her life, her research, her life on the phone.

Fortunately it turns out that she is very good on the phone. She has been amazed at how much information is accessible that way, thanks to just the right blend of practicality, cheekiness, charm. There are men all over the city who love it when she calls, even the way she ticks them off if they're too fast, too dry, not clear. It's fun for them, being the expert on the phone, in their offices. Maybe they have paunches, zits, eleven children; she'll never know.

She does not go out in the evenings, either, except to AA. And last night she quit that. It's been a year. How much public bloodletting can anyone need?

Kate pauses at the curb, makes sure her handbag is safely slung across her shoulder underneath her fringed cashmere shawl, feels for the notebook inside. She has an appointment with a Detective-Sergeant Smeeth – whose job, astoundingly, seems to be not much more than that of briefing filmmakers and writers. When she finally got him on the line, Kate made some little jest about this, something about how nice it was that for once public money was being spent on *imaginary* crime – the sort of remark her father might have made with heavy irony, though of course Kate meant it strictly in the lighthearted way. His voice was dry and resistant to her whimsy. He did not, he said, discuss any sort of crime on the phone. She would have to come down to his office at the station, then he would see what he could do. It made her think of walnuts, that voice – of how you can stick a knife blade into the crack and sometimes pry apart the shell. Before she left her apartment she took off a floppy hat, and put it on, and took it off again.

This street is truly creepy. It is full of eyes, even though no one looks at her. Kate is wearing a tartan dress with twenty black jet buttons, high boots with chunky heels, that cashmere shawl, her bracelet of gold charms. Her parents began the bracelet the year she was born. At school she wore it even for badminton and cheerleading and algebra exams. She makes sure the bracelet is safely tucked within her sleeve.

This is a chill March afternoon. Gusts of cloud, needles of sun. In front of the Brandiz Hotel a man in a plaid shirt and base-ball cap is hosing down the sidewalk, and water is spraying up the front of his jeans, soaking his shoes. Kate edges by, carefully, and then skirts the pub of the Roosevelt, next door, which shares an entrance with a steam room and a video arcade. She takes out her notebook . . . *shares an entrance with a steam room and a video arcade.* A bottle crashes from a window across the street.

"Looking for a place to stay?"

She whirls around. The man who has come up beside her has faded blue eyes with a pinkish overlay.

"Because this isn't where you should look – it's all cock-roach heaven along here. This is the most dangerous strip in North America," he says.

Do I *look* like a candidate for cockroach heaven? she demands in a silent voice that is well-intentioned, even amused, though edged with a chill that could set anyone back on his heels. *Wobbly poached eyes*, she notes in her head. Still, if the point of this foray has been to soak in real street atmosphere, shouldn't she buy this man a coffee? She almost laughs, because isn't this the perfect chance to work at regaining the skill of interacting, as Fred the therapist was constantly urging, before she canned him. "*Katie, I've never met anyone who smiles so much, and holds herself so closed . . . !*" The man is keeping step beside her, anyway. "Go on across Main a block or two," he's insisting. "But along this strip, forget it! Believe me, I should know." He is unzipping the front of his windbreaker, which is made of some sort of silver stuff. He is flapping it open, drawing her attention to a badge sewn on the front. "Look at this – this is *Guardia Civil*," fingering a fuzzy oval about the size of a mango, with Chinese letters sewn in black, "this is the official uniform," staring at her hard, trying to make sure she understands. "Fuck it, you wouldn't believe the fucking stories I could tell you – those bastards have got their grips on every country, it's a fucking scandal. But listen, the minute we get word from Barcelona we're moving in."

What does it mean when the crazies seek you out to pass on their secrets? Kate gets a most peculiar feeling walking along-side this man, as if she could hear the clicking of the atoms of an alternate universe, every planet whirling in its groove, music revealed to very few.

She gives her head a shake, wobbling her curls. Now she's passing a bunch of men standing around the stairs to the urinal by the Carnegie Centre, and she dodges across the street though the light has turned red, and hurries east along Main, checking her reflection in the windows of the BFK Novelty Shop, the Golden Harvest Cinema, the Needle Exchange.

She is a good twenty minutes early. She sits down on a bus-stop bench, to pull herself together. She jumps to her feet again, A man is lying underneath. He takes a slug from a bottle in a paper bag, and then rolls over, his face squashed into the shoulder of the curb.

And Kate smells Charlie, suddenly. The way her cheek would come to rest above his armpit, the way she would breathe security from that dank hollow: the way his breath would turn sharp, metallic, after he'd taken her briskly in the dark.

All the choices she has made this past year are ridiculous, she sees. She is exactly the person she was before, only she has spent almost four hundred nights without any human being touching her. All her stupid pride, all that pretending she's about to do some great redeeming thing – what a hoax. She stands outside the Sunshine Cafe, picking at her cuticles, gnawing at a strip that's torn away, and she sees herself crawling back, flattening right out on the floor. *Step on me. Please.*

~

Detective-Sergeant Smeeth's office is windowless and filled with metal, the chairs and desk and carpet done in shades of handcuff grey. John Smeeth. Call me John. She is dismayed at her own lack of inventiveness, for she would never have dreamed up such a man, yet he is absolutely right: waxy faced and crafty, a man who understands exactly how the cogs fit the wheels. He crosses the room with a limp, but he looks pumped up with fitness, in a subterranean way. Those murky eyes, those arms as thick as firehoses, very rubbery and pale. He offers to take Kate's wrap. He blinks and then recovers as her bracelet clatters against the metal of her chair. He is doing a complete inventory, too, as if all her parts were on a tray for him to memorize – for official purposes, that's the most generous construction.

He settles back behind the desk. "So where exactly does this murder take place?" He removes a cigarette from a pack of unfiltered Players, taps it, stretches back in his chair with his hands folded across his stomach, the unlit cigarette poking out from between his balled-up fingers, just below the belt.

If he lights that, I am going to object, Kate is thinking. Though perhaps it would be better lit than where it is.

She catches herself digging both hands into her hair, giving clumps of it a pull. Then she laughs, spreads her hands. "I guess I'm a little nervous. My murder? In fact not far from here."

"A Chinatown murder. Good."

"Well, not exactly. I'm thinking of an old building over on Powell. I work in a jam factory over there – just down from the strip club on the corner. Number Five Orange, I mean."

Just down from the strip club on the corner. She didn't have to say that.

He raises an eyebrow. "So you must work for the famous Jenny. Quite a well-known Chinatown figure, all the same. Fire department, health department, you name it – they've all had sample cases of Jenny's jams. Of course that can't have any-thing to do with the fact the building's up to be condemned."

Kate has to laugh. The way she was brought up, it is absolutely fundamental to laugh whenever a laugh is called for. "You're not saying Jenny's trying to buy city hall with preserves?"

Smeeth's lower eyelids pull up like the rims of a bird's eyes, shoring in dark distasteful knowledge of the way things really are. "So what do *you* find to do in that sticky place, Ms. Rutherford?" He is studying her hands, the bitten cuticles, the fingers scored with sewing-needle marks, maybe even the absence of a ring. "Hey, I have it. Jenny dresses up her jams jars, doesn't she? And you're the one who sews those little apron things. I've always wondered who they got to do that sort of work."

"Well, in fact –"

"And you plan your murders while you sew. I bet you're writing your boss in as the corpse."

"Oh, heavens – I'm just borrowing her premises, you might say."

"Come on, I know how you writers always get the last word in. She has you on piecework, right? Which works out to about fifty cents an hour. You're not trying to support the kids on that, I hope."

"*Kids?* Perish the thought."

Of course that is not what she means. But now, because of how it came out like a disavowal, Charlie's voice barges in. *"Perish the thought, indeed. There is no judge in the country who would let you within a mile of those kids! What if they'd been in the car? The fact that so far you have managed not to murder any of my children is just a fucking miracle!"*

And Smeeth is also looking stern. "But you do have three of the little nippers? Correct?" He reaches over and just barely touches her charm bracelet. His stubby finger has a moon-shaped bruise beneath the nail.

Oh you big fat ass, she wants to say, *leave my children out of this*. But she has to fight the urge to get down on her knees. Everything about this stern grey room prompts abasement. *Do you know how thin a baby's skull is?* she could say. *Anything could happen – bricks could fall out of the sky. And that fear goes on and on for years. Do you have any idea what that fear can do to you?* That is the sort of thing she used to say to Fred the therapist, and he would blink his lovely puzzled eyes.

"I see an itty-bitty cradle," Smeeth is saying, the back of a finger grazing the charms, ". . . and here's a pair of booties . . . and here's a christening mug engraved with. . . ." He peers closer. "Kyle?"

"Is this a lesson in detection?" Kate keeps the smile in her voice, but pulls her arm away. She doesn't catch his reply, for now it is Kyle's voice she hears. *Please, Mum, please, please, please – we don't want to lose all respect for you . . . !*

Kyle. Her sweet oldest boy, having to say that on behalf of his brother and his sister. And he is doing what now, because of her? Turning to dope because of her? Listening to music that rots his soul? Charlie will never know what's going on – look how he never had the faintest clue what was going on inside of her. What *was* going on inside of her?

Maybe Smeeth reads some of what she's thinking. "Kids!" he says. "Boy! Hostages to fortune, eh?" She sees that he, too, has a groove on his finger where a ring used to be. Then he settles back with that cigarette balled up in his fingers again. "So, Ms. Rutherford – confess. I'd say you're just doing that jam job to collect atmosphere."

"Well you'd jolly well be wrong."

He widens his eyes, tilts his head. He shows a gap between his front teeth when he smiles. "No Mr. Rutherford?"

"*Doctor* Rutherford, please."

"No Doctor Rutherford, then?"

"Not since he pushed me down the stairs."

She can't imagine why she said that. She has never mentioned that to anyone. The fact that she dashed out immediately after and smashed Charlie's car up cancelled it out, in a way. But if she had to think about it, which she doesn't, it would still be the thing that fills her most with a peculiar feeling she can hardly get a handle on. No, not anger. No, no, no – her therapist had been completely wrong – not even shame. When Fred finally pried the story out of her, he said, "Katie, come on – it's absolutely standard for the victim to blot out something like that because of shame." Fred. She loved him so much by then she could not bear to embarrass him by pointing out how he was wrong, how the moment Charlie pushed her down the stairs had been the most thrilling moment of her life, in a way. Thinking of that, she starts picking at her cuticle again.

"Hey, say no more," Smeeth is saying. "So the doctor disappears, so what else is new? I forgot – you're in the murder business."

"Then you're not going to read me my rights?"

"On Doctor Rutherford you get a freebie," Smeeth says.

Oh he's quick, this detective. Kate had forgotten the pure pleasure of words flicked back and forth, but all this is coming back to her, the way at moments like this you can achieve an almost Zen-like rightness. Of course the man is way beyond the pale, as her father used to say. That short-sleeved shirt, the undershirt showing through. The shirt is pushed out flat and hard. What's underneath must be rocklike. "Marmoreal" is the word that comes to her, what a fine sinister word. Smeeth's chunky arms are hairless, white as marble. His chest must be too. You could roll a pie out on that chest.

"So, now let me get this straight," Smeeth is saying. "We've got this dead lady floating in a vat of blackberry jam . . . ?"

She feels a prick of paranoia, for indeed this is exactly her opening scene. Maybe the interest she sensed is not in *her* at all – maybe this man lurks in the depths of the police station like a fat white spider, waiting to prey on the imaginations of those who come to him for help. She scans his shelves. A dictionary (Webster's), also a thesaurus, and next to that *The Elements of Style*. Has she given away too much already?

"Too bad," Smeeth is saying. "Because that would be a beauty. I mean, from the police point of view. You could pinpoint the time of death just by the colour of her skin. Here, I'll give you the number of a guy over in forensic in case you change your mind. But, hang on a tick! Now I get it. It's the jam-maker who figures everything *out*, am I right? She's not the victim after all. She's the one with all the expertise that's going to run circles round the cops. Oh, you writers – I don't know why we don't come to *you*."

This is scary, but it's also like dancing in a way. Look how his mind moves with hers, as if he could reach out and pick her thoughts from the air. Yes, her imaginary sleuth does have exactly the wiles and cranky charm of her boss Jenny (though Jenny will lose a decade, gain a black silk dress slit from hem to thigh). Has he also figured out the identity of the body in the jam? – that Kate, herself, is that lovely floating body, turning blue? And that the villain is Charlie? – the reconstructive surgeon who in the search for perfection has gone one step too far – only to be undone by a woman no one even stops to think has brains, who has the sort of accent that makes people speak very loudly in reply – and who does, indeed, run rings around the police. Kate is almost moved to share all of this with Smeeth, so they could laugh together at his cleverness and hers.

She allows him just the slim edge of the smile her mother kept for putting people in their place. She taps her pen on her notebook. "What I need to know, precisely, is the procedure once the body is found. Who comes to the scene? How does it go?"

Smeeth slides up an eyebrow. "What time?"

"Nine in the morning."

"Oh excellent. You'll have a new shift, all alert and bushy-tailed. Someone calls 911 of course; then a couple of beat constables hoof it over and confirm. Why not make one of *them* Chinese as well?"

"As well as what?"

He shrugs. "I'd play up the Chinatown angle, that's all. Push the local colour – don't forget you're going to want to flog the movie rights."

The movie rights! As if this were the obvious next move, not her most impossible wild dream.

"So tell me," she says, brushing the movie rights aside, "if a second murder was reported the same day, it might seem likely there's a connection?"

"If you put it in, there's bound to be." He gives this the happy look a snake might give a rabbit. "Where's *this* body discovered, by the way?"

"The . . . bandshell at English Bay?"

"Ah, that will be a radio car that gets that. I'd put a woman in the car, play up the feminine angle. She calls in to the chief of homicide and he says, 'Oh shit, another one . . . !'"

Oh shit, another one. . . . She starts scribbling frantically, trying to get down every blessed thing he says. It comes to her that he is treating her as a true professional, that maybe he believes she's who she says. A lovely furry feeling overcomes her as she details how the scene at the jam factory will be secured, the photos taken, the body whisked away. It reminds her of all those times she stood and slowly turned while her mother put pins in the hem of a dress for her. A man who listens or a man who talks, just fine either way. No wonder she fell in love with Fred, who listened to every lying word she had to say. For a second, as she scribbles, she sees how it is all about trust, how the key to everything must be to crack open even if it hurts. Why, if she'd been brave enough she could even have linked up with an imaginary chapter of the *Guardia Civil*, and got herself a secret badge and bright metallic uniform. Perhaps that crazy man was a sign. She could have smiled at him, at least. She does not always have to be above the world. As she takes down what Smeeth details, she is also trying to isolate the smells in this room. The artificial-fibre carpet is the strongest. Smeeth gives off no smell at all. The carpet must be new; it gives off a smell like chloroform. Imagine having your nose squashed into that, the harsh grey twists against your cheek and brow and chin. *Zipped up in plastic body bags . . .* she is writing *. . . removed to the morgue.*

"And then the body gets placed in the columbarium," Smeeth says. "Now there's a word for you." He waits till she looks up. "That's the room with all the sliding cooler trays."

Something has changed. She feels some rearrangement of the molecules between them. He is expecting her to ask something. Columbarium. All the murdered people, labelled, sealed in plastic, padlocked into steel compartments. If she asked, would he take her there? Does he want to take her there? Smeeth waits, expressionless, head cocked to the side. She is aware of that split between his teeth. She is aware of the small glistening point of his tongue. She feels buoyant, giddy, wary, her bones stuffed with something that is either excitement or disdain, making her springy as a deer. But he will have to ask her decently. (Kate's mother puts the final stitches in a hem, and Kate's date waits below, and Kate takes a twirl.)

The detective glances at his watch, ejects a small final-sounding breath. "Well, so then you'll proceed to the autopsy," he says.

She has lost him. She remembers the signs of this exactly, how one minute everything you say is right and the next they can hardly wait to get you off their hands. It is a miracle that Charlie whisked her off to Spanish Banks the night that she got chosen Homecoming Queen, and removed the crown and all the rest and she didn't have to say a word.

"And then of course you'll have an inquest," Smeeth is saying. "For example – here's a case that's still unsolved." He swivels back, brings down a file from the shelf behind him. "This is the complete story of an investigation, right here."

A hard-board binder with rings the size of jar lids, the pages surprisingly tattered and brown. The whole thing looks so well-thumbed in fact that Kate feels a warning shiver, not without excitement. *Wait! – he just pretends to pick a file at random, but this is the one he uses every time.* She finds herself leaning forward with an odd sense of complicity.

"Nice drama," Smeeth says. "Listen." He starts reading out dialogue from an actual inquest. He reads the testimony of the beat constable – how the deceased, Mrs. Juanita Alvarez, was found lying in an alley. He reads the testimony of the doctor – how the knife entered through the chest and again through the stomach: thrusts so powerful they emerged through the lower back. Now he unclips the rings and removes half a dozen glossy photographs. He lays these out across the desk where Kate can see. He sits back, and finally lights his cigarette.

Juanita Alvarez is young. Her skin is very white, her nipples black. Her death is so stark in these black-and-white shots; her body is so lovely otherwise. Just below the breasts, and then again across the soft flesh above her pubic hair, two puckered gashes have been sewn with coarse black thread.

This one's still unsolved. Kate hears the way Smeeth says that, again and again, each time the girl is exposed.

How many times has she been laid out here? Smeeth exhales a rush of nicotine that shoots across the desk, bringing his breath with it too. How many times, exactly at this juncture, has he sat back to light his cigarette? Is this a well-known syndrome, the voltage that burns through Kate's body as she looks at the pictures of the girl? She is imagining Smeeth's squat hands, his stubby fingers, his awful whiteness – like those plants that you can drink from in the desert if you're dying, the pale rubber of their skin, the bitter release of sickly fluid. If he got up and came around the desk now, she would do any fucking thing he wanted – and what kind of person can she be if that is what such pictures do to her?

$\sim$

She stops walking, finally. She has no idea what to think.

She was only a beat too late, back there. "Oh . . .!" she said, into that congealed atmosphere. "Oh yes, I see – the knife goes through the rib cage, does it? That must require quite a thrust. The killer would have to be a man, wouldn't you say?"

She asked all the proper questions. If she ever looks into her notebook again, it will all be there.

Smeeth walked her to the elevator, too – and at the last minute jumped in and rode right down with her. "Here, let me give you this," he said. "Maybe you'll be sitting in the middle of the night, and you'll need something right away. Who knows?" He wrote his home phone number on the cover of her notebook crammed with details about bullet angles and strangulation marks and the length of time a body takes to cool.

Now she stands absolutely still in the middle of the late-afternoon crowd on Main Street, unaware of people jostling her. *You build things up, and they fall down. That is life's entire plot.*

Someone is looking at her. Someone sees exactly the way shame wells through her body with a force that is going to melt her bones. A man is shuffling towards her, leaning on a cane, a disintegrating man, his skin watery, bloated – though he could be young, he could be Charlie's age. Why is he looking at her as if he knows her? So familiar, that expression – as if he had trailed

her all this year, as if he had oozed after her across the wasteland
of withdrawal, as if he was another of those apparitions that had
conjured themselves up out of the aching lack of drink as she lay
trembling, wide-awake, in the hospital last year.

But this is a person. This is a fellow human being, and now he
is peering at her through glasses so thick they are almost yellow,
as if he has something important to say.

What does she do to attract these people? Could every bizarre
encounter of today have been some sort of trick inside her head,
even the seamy aspects of her interview with Smeeth? – a
product of her needy warped imagination, which can never
accept things as they are but must always make them worse?

Maybe Smeeth was a perfectly nice man, just trying to do his
job. Maybe he was as lonely as she was.

What if she did call him, late one night? Late one night,
from the morgue-like silence of her room, what if she got him on
the line?

Now this damaged man has stopped right in front of her.

Of course. He wants money. He is not here to reveal some
further dismal fact about herself. Money is all he wants.

All she has is a twenty-dollar bill, and bus fare – all she has in
the world until she gets the current batch of aprons done. Well
then! She will give him everything she has. This thought has
trouble squeezing out, but it leaves her limp and saved. The gift
will be for herself, of course, in the manner of most offerings.

"Excuse me," he says, "could you just help me across that
corner down there?" He points back in the direction of the
police station. "I have to get to the bus stop."

So he is here to point out a further lack in her, after all. For
look how she recoils. Why her? *Why me!* Why not those busi-
nessmen in pinstripes who have just sidled out of Number Five,
one with his fly undone?

She thinks what her mother would have done. Without one
moment's hesitation, even dead and gone, her mother would
pass by on the other side.

She tucks her bracelet up inside her sleeve, holds out her arm.

The man reaches barely to her ear, but before she has a chance
to resist he forces his arm through hers and grabs her hand.

This is a strength she knows from dreams. His hand settles into hers, palm to palm, such an intimate connection. His thick eyes goggle up at her.

"Do you have trouble seeing?" she asks. "Is that why you need help?"

"No," he says simply. "I have trouble walking. I'm afraid I'll fall down."

A bus pulls away from that far stop. "I hope that wasn't *your* bus," she says.

"It doesn't matter. Any bus will do. I only came down here for the meeting. I'm trying to break a really bad addiction. Fifteen years. Every time I get clear, I go under again."

Oh lord, and the man reeks of years of desolation, a smell so hollow and awful it has the strength of an undertow – and floating on the top of that, the sweet dank odour of an afternoon spent drinking beer.

This is crazy. His breath is misting up her cheek. His hand rests in hers, like a small hot animal. *Every time I get clear, I go under again.* She has walked with her children just this way. They will never remember that, now. She would have given her lifeblood for them. Did that prevent her from doing things so weak and ugly it will take them their whole lives to get over her? And look at this man, reeking of beer.

She stops and jerks her arm free. He will never get clear. What is the point of getting clear? Even sober and straight he will still be a half-blind cripple, afraid of falling down. She gives him a fast fake smile as he stands wobbling there. "I'm sorry. I just realized I'm late for an appointment." He is staring, meekly, as if he'd known from the start this was what she'd do. Then she catches something further in his expression, something sly.

Her hand is sticky where he held it. She walks away very fast. Some dreadful sticky substance has transferred itself from his hand to hers, and she can feel those raw places on her fingers, all that shredded skin, those little half-healed wounds. Oh Jesus, she says, Oh ugh, Oh Christ. She will have to go straight over to Jenny's and scrub her hands with bleach.

She almost runs across the street, against the yellow light. But when she gets to the other side she has to turn and look back. He is exactly where she left him, staring after her. He raises that hand.

~

Shadows take on a different character at a certain time of afternoon. I deal in shadows, but even I find that so. I have just spent six months of my life capturing shadows with my camera, then marshalling them into patterns, turning those patterns into stencils, printing the stencils onto silk. It seemed a good thing, at that time of my life (I began the project when I had recently left what I had thought was love behind) to be able to tame shadows. The order I sent off to New York this afternoon contained the whole of those months' work, fifteen bolts printed with the webbed and tangling silhouettes of huckleberry, mountain ash, alder leaves, ferns. Now the shadow of my piano is a flattened tongue, advancing slowly across my bare hardwood floor.

I can imagine how shadows looked to Kate that afternoon on Main Street, shadows flopping over curbs, peeling onto the road, becoming slick dark conduits that might carry you along. Don't all of us suspect there's a place you could broach if you only had the nerve and the light was right? You walk an echoing corridor that spirals down. You enter a locked room. Wonder of wonders, everything is labelled; you just need to find the right drawer, slit the plastic, and at last you're face to face with who you are. Then, instead, imagine staring in and in and finding merely a lack so great that all the sweetness of the world is not enough. Nothing will fill this, though of course you have to try.

When Charlie pushed her down the stairs, it seemed that Kate had been awaiting just such a final thing for years. Look at him, cracking free of his shell of irreproachable behaviour at last. Every unhappiness she had known or imagined was finally justified in that moment when Charlie grabbed her by the shoulders shouting, *Why are you doing this, why, why,* why? That was the shame of it, that was what scared her – that she could exert such power and bring it crashing back upon herself, and for one moment feel truly alive. That was what she could never tell the therapist.

And Charlie wanted her back, that was another thing she never told. He wanted her back no matter what. She would be able to do anything, drink oceans, have delusions, goodness knows. She was his wife. He was a responsible man of medicine. From now on though, forever, he would never again pay Kate the attention that he paid her the day he pushed her down the stairs.

Against all of that, she has spent her whole year of freedom struggling. She has stored up not just boxes of details about crime, but words, treasure chests of words that any day she will melt into shining sentences. Sometimes, when she has been doing other things, those words have arranged themselves. Sometimes she has dropped what she's been doing, taken out her typewriter, put a fresh piece of paper in, keeping her eye on the lovely artifact that has just appeared before her eyes – that product of *her* mind, hers – a sudden glimmer through the silt of her everyday concerns. But every time she has plunged in to take it, she has come up with a dented hubcap, or an old rubber boot.

Disgusting, awful, awful, Kate says, as she hurries along Main Street, away from the crippled man. What a mess in the end, this day – harassed by madmen and lewd policemen, and shamed into giving her arm to perverts with god knows what on their hands. Such a dupe she was – so unable to refuse, so superstitious. So afraid of falling down. But she is reaching out for all that now, she is gathering it in. Awful, awful. Look how she's tried and tried, and look where she is. The air around her glitters with triumphant awfulness, final as when her husband last put his hands on her. No one should have to suffer this.

At Jenny's she will ask for money. This is not the impulse of a moment – no, she understands, all at once, that it has been in her head all day long, a clever plan of escape should the day go wrong. And look at her, a jittering wreck, useless to the world; twenty dollars is never going to get her where she needs to go.

At Jenny's she will plead dire emergency, maybe a family illness in a foreign city like Toronto, requiring a round-trip ticket, a considerable sum. She starts calculating odds. If she asks Jenny for five hundred, will she end up with three? Well, she thinks, I can even pawn my bracelet come to that.

She has started shaking, but that hardly matters, it's just a stage along the way. Her veins flood with the splendid golden weakness of this moment where she's arrived, without thought or conscious choice, right on the other side of all the barriers.

And as for me, I killed my child so I could keep my lover. That is the short story of my life.

He did not make me do it. "Look, it's your decision," was all he said, "but you can't . . ." (his anguished persecuted look), ". . . surely you do not expect me to stay around and help you raise it, that's all. You have always known how I felt."

Yes, I had certainly known that he had a horror of other people's children. It wasn't just the noise and fuss, it was a more basic fear than that. He felt the very essence of himself assaulted by the small shrill voices and the clutter of baby packs and strollers and fuzzy toys and soothers that, one by one, the few couples we were friends with had succumbed to. "We have a perfect life, Mariel," he'd often said as he fled some gathering of colleagues and their partners, the fathers with snugglies on their chests, *like goddamn emasculated kangaroos*, as he put it, "how thankful I am for the calm and sanity of the life I lead with you."

He was my husband of seven years, this man I still speak of as my lover. He was a solitary man, and when we met I felt such a jolt of recognition – as if I'd had the extraordinary luck of coming upon a missing part of myself – that I became his double as nearly as I could. I allowed him to build a cage for me out of air, and for seven years I sheltered there. I thought that if he ever left me I would die.

Of course I did not try to conceive a child. After a time I began to believe, in any case, that no baby would be kind enough to come and rest in that dry sack of mine. I was completely unprepared for the shock of life settling inside me. It was only then I understood that I had forgotten there was even such a thing as joy.

No, he did not make me do it. But after I had done it, I could not stand to look at his essential face again.

That is an old story now. I try not to dwell on it. I work. Usually I thank whatever fates there are that I have the need to do this, and that I am good at what I do. I work, and live alone. I was never pretty. I recognize that there is no escape for me. Still, I can't give up the hope that out of the patience and skill and care my narrow life requires, will come the thing that saves me – grace, I suppose I mean.

Sometimes though, on days like this, I wish I had the courage to abandon hope completely – to imagine, if even for a moment, that I might just let go and blaze and burn, and it wouldn't matter after that, nothing would matter; I would rise from the ashes, or not. It would be completely out of my hands.

And so I watch Kate Rutherford, at the close of that chill March afternoon. She has taken a taxi from the jam factory back to the west side of the city. I see her stand for a moment on the curb, trying to give the impression of a woman unhurried, normal, calm. I watch as she follows the driver up the stairs to her tiny dim apartment. He sets a carton by the phone. Will she ask him to stay? It will never cross her mind. She will be trembling, but she will take the time to look into the mirror, where she will see herself as merry and beautiful and bad.

The door will close. The first bottle will be opened. And words will flow through her like a serum, and the room will fill with evening with no one to turn on the light, only Kate, floating like a lily, borne upon the surface of that delicious murmuring.

LINDA LITTLE

The Still

Jackson's bootleg business was open any hour you could rouse him. He lived an inner solitude so profound he remained untouched by the constant flow and swirl of his clientele. He sat to the side, said nothing, offered an enigmatic smile if pressed for an opinion. Jackson was an excellent bootlegger. He kept a reasonable selection of commercial product but realized his best profit from the manufacture and sale of untaxed alcohol. He kept half a dozen kegs full of home-brew and made wine that could light a barbecue. He was an alcoholic. He understood alcoholics.

The smell of bacon frying prodded Jackson awake. He wasn't alone in his cabin. He didn't care to think that through immediately. He buried his face into his pillow, eyes still closed, and took stock of his body. At twenty-eight years old it held up well to abuse, recovered quickly. He wasn't too bad. He shuffled himself around so he could lean over the edge of the bed and grope through the case of Keith's he kept under there. When his hand located a full bottle he sat up in bed, plumping the pillows behind him, and sipped back his hair-of-the-dog like a Victorian lady taking her tonic. It was Lori, he remembered, who was frying the bacon.

Lori always woke up first. She wanted a chance to fix her face. Not the whole story; she didn't want to appear desperate. Just enough to fix her colour, hide any bags under the eyes, maybe a touch of liner. She wanted to give her hair that sexy tousled look. She chose her blue flip-flops and a workshirt of Jackson's, carefully rolling up the sleeves and pulling it together with just the two middle buttons. She had seen Demi Moore in a magazine once in a workshirt. It looked like she had no underwear or anything and the shirt could fall off at any second.

Jackson sat over his breakfast trying to bring into focus an idea he had been working on yesterday. He piled his bacon onto the toast to build a sandwich. His eggs had all the whites cut off them, three golden buttons, cooked all the way through so they didn't run. He blinked in embarrassment that Lori knew this about him. The old Surge milking machine! That was what he had been thinking about. And copper piping looped around and around through cold water in that sink. His eyes shone.

Lori, leaning back against the sink, caught the hungry gleam in his eye. She raised her fingers to her hair. "I always look a fright in the morning," she giggled.

He had wine nearly ready. He could start with that, to try. Move to a cheaper mash later on. He licked his lips.

Lori giggled again. She sauntered over to him and wriggled her way onto his lap. "You were terrific last night."

Jackson noticed her there on his lap. He mumbled, as always, into his beard. "Good breakfast." Her chest was so close he had to turn his head to finish his toast. He could heat the mash on his hot plate. Or maybe a Coleman would be better?

"I cleaned up a bit," she said. "This is not a bad place. It's so cool that you built it yourself. I used to go out with this other guy, I mean like *years* ago, and he was so useless you wouldn't believe. He got a flat tire once and I had to change it for him . . ."

Jackson was thinking about soldering. "I'd want a blowtorch for that job," he may have said. Lori slid onto her knees on the floor in front of him.

The barn was down at the road, next to his mother's house where he and his nine brothers and sisters had been raised. His mom still kept an old Jersey and a couple of beef but mostly the pigeons had taken over, dropping long furrows of shit onto old hay beneath the beams. Piles of junk had grown up in the centre of the barn. Jackson picked through it, quickly coming across the main part of the milker, a large, round, stainless-steel container with a plate-sized hole in the top where the cover fit. Finding the cover was the hard part, it being so much smaller. An hour into the search the only things of value he had unearthed were a ball cap he had lost some years ago, a Robertson screwdriver, and his brother, Matthew, passed out on a bed of mouldy straw. He might have given up except that Matthew gave a groan and twisted his body. An arc of steel glinted from underneath his armpit. Jackson reached under his brother to pull out the missing piece. There was a hay fork under there too, which looked uncomfortable, so he pulled that out as well. Fitted together, the milker looked like a huge silver curling stone.

Lori picked up the beer bottles and spot-cleaned the painted aspenite floor where there had been spills. She gathered up the piles of shavings in the corner where Jackson sat to whittle. She swept. She emptied the hubcap ashtrays. She wiped the table and little squares of counter at each end of the sink. Next time she would bring some vinegar to do the window, maybe borrow a brush from Rosie and give the floor a good scrub. Linoleum flooring would be better. The walls were yellow with tobacco smoke but it was hard to wash chipboard that hadn't been painted. She would wallpaper them if they were hers, and make some curtains for the window and put in a little cookstove there instead of that old pot belly. She made the bed but that was hard too because the bedroom was hardly bigger than the bed. She blushed a little at the grey pallor of the sheets. Jackson had a tiny bathroom with cold running water but he'd never got around to hooking up the toilet. So it sat there, taking up half the space, the bowl crammed with empty beer bottles, several cases of homebrew stacked on the tank. She wiped out the sink, rubbing the amber stains until they glowed.

It had been almost a year now that she had been "dropping by," visiting Rosie, wandering back to see Jackson, waiting around for successive tribes of boisterous drunks to finish their business and drive off, packed like sardines into the cabs of their rickety pickups. It had been almost a year since the first time, the night they had both been so drunk. It had been easier after that. If she was there when everyone else had left he might reach out and stroke her thigh or squeeze her waist. He had lovely big hands. Strong. He said so little it was hard to tell what he was thinking. But he had never been mean to her. Ever. And he had given her three of his carvings. She had a lonely-looking raven and a spruce tree and an odd one of a bottle with a gnarled old hand gripping it.

By eleven o'clock Jackson's breathing was becoming laboured. It was the pressure against the emptiness. Jackson felt his ribcage harden into a tin cylinder. There was nothing inside. Nothing. Whenever he spoke to other people it was like climbing up out of a well. It was hard to focus on them, they were so far away, at the wrong end of a telescope. He had to put them together in his mind, piece by piece. He had to strain to hear them over the rush of nothingness. The muted mumblings he produced required great effort, as if he were shouting across a chasm, shouts usually lost in an echo before they reached anyone. It was too much work.

Jackson would have one beer when he woke up in the morning, two if he really needed them. After that, he held out for the rest of the morning, as long as he could, until his chest started to crinkle under an irresistible pressure, like an empty beer can in a closing fist. Then he would drink. It was like pouring water into that can, filling the vacuum, packing substance into the void, relieving the pressure.

He left his milker by the farmhouse, in the tool shack they had always flattered with the term "workshop." He headed back to his cabin. The seashell drone in his ears had become a roar. He drew himself a pitcher of homebrew from the keg, drank it straight down, draining the pitcher. Lori perched on the edge of a rickety chair, filing her nails and chattering away a mile a minute. Then she looked at him expectantly, waiting for a response. He smiled, hoping that would pass as an answer. He drew off another pitcher. Since Lori had washed all the glasses that had been lying around he had to search the shelves for some. He poured them each a beer.

She giggled, uncertain. "What's that smile supposed to mean?" She sounded rickety, half way between hopeful and humiliated. "Do you want to get married or not?" She had wanted it to sound strong and "no nonsense" like Rosie, but it came out more like a plea. And she could feel the tears welling up in her eyes.

Jackson understood that she was talking to him, about him. About them. But it was like overhearing a conversation in a laundromat. He took another long drink then picked up the owl he was carving.

She couldn't believe she had started this and wished to god she could go back. Then a whoop and a holler and a burst of ribald laughter rolled into the air between them. Jackson's first customers of the day had arrived. She had never felt so alone.

"I'm not hanging around while that crowd drools all over your floor! I'm going to Rosie's to call my sister to come and pick me up." She was leaking tears now. "Oh, Jacky, I love you!" She hugged his neck as he stood by the doorway waiting for his customers.

Jackson put his hands on her waist. He could see, dispassionately, how he could have bedded her all those times. 'Doggy style,' he thought and the expression brought a tiny smile to his lips. She looked up at him, into that faint, shy smile searching for her dignity. She grabbed her things and fled.

Jackson stooped over his work in the tool shed by the farmhouse, forming a length of bendable copper piping, curling it around and around in perfect, even loops. While he worked he forced himself to think about Lori. It was like doing a school math problem, completely apart from him. Academic. It made no sense that she would want to marry him but she did. It didn't make any difference to him. Nothing did. He didn't want to upset anyone. If it would make her happy . . . He had no experience with this kind of thing. And he wasn't fond of metal work. Soldering and welding made him feel far from his hands.

He didn't notice his four- and five-year-old nephews until a little fist curled around the pipe.

"Jackson's making a giant-size slinky!"

Matthew sauntered along behind his boys. He leaned on the doorpost, watching progress. "Never you mind that, Old Man," he said to his son. "And don't you two get into any trouble or I'll whoop yez both." The boys paid no attention.

"I'll give you a hand with the solder later on if you want." Jackson nodded at his lap. When Jackson heard receding footsteps on the gravel he looked up and watched his brother stroll off, shoulders swaying gracefully on his lanky frame.

When Lori started her period she did her very best to feel relieved. The relief, though, floated on the surface of a deep pool of desperation. By the end of the day she had locked her sister out of their tiny room and lay across her bed weeping. She simply could not bear it if one more person looked past her to choose a bottle. Jackson had to love her. She did everything right. She never asked him for anything. Until today. Why did she say that? Why? 'I love you, Jacky. Want to marry me?' She spat the sentences out over and over in a stream of rarefied venom. She buried her face in her pillow where she sobbed. "Stupid-stupid-stupid. Stupid!" Eventually, her sister's angry pounding on the door roused her. She took her time getting up. Maybe my thighs are too fat, she thought. Nobody wants to marry a big fat cow.

Matthew showed up for the soldering and the inaugural run. When they'd finished tinkering with the joints, Matthew held the milker while Jackson poured in the wine. Soon the still had settled into operation and they sat back to wait and watch.

"Good thing it's you and me, b'y," Matthew crowed. "Cause brandy's too good for that regular crowd you got around here."

Jackson looked across the table at his brother, saw the way his hair twirled in a cowlick above his left eye, the tiny scar beside his nose where he'd been hit with a snowball filled with ice as a kid. He looked, for just a second, into his eyes. He couldn't remember the last time he'd looked into the eyes of another human being and the intensity of it stung him. He gathered himself up.

"Lori wants to get married."

"Wow. Is she pregnant?"

The question had never occurred to Jackson. Now that he thought of it he supposed it was possible.

"I don't know."

"Well, you better ask her, buddy! Jesus, Jackson, sometimes I think you're thick like that." He rapped on the wooden table-top with his knuckles.

Jackson got up and checked the connections in the still.

"Married. Christ, I remember before me and Rosie got married, when we were going out. What a time we had. We went up to that barbecue in Scotsburn. Remember I told you that time ole stunned arse, Clifford, was selling hash in the parking lot? And he was so lit he thought he was putting it back in the glove compartment of his car but really it was the minister's car? And the minister and his wife came back and drove off and Clifford took off running down the road after them, cussing a blue streak? Rosie hates that fucker, Clifford. She near pissed herself that day she laughed so hard.

"And remember that time Barry Landry was working for Van Dyke and he got fired cause he fucked off and never fed the pigs? And he was pissed off because he never got his last day's pay. So we all rattled over there in Barry's old truck and stole those piglets and ran out of gas and the Mountie came up and Rosie had to convince him we're home late from the sale? Home from the cattle sale at three o'clock in the fuckin' morning!? She was beautiful. I didn't care when she got pregnant. I was glad. I'd've married her the first day I met her."

The still chortled and gave out a low hiss.

Matthew's voice turned oddly warm and delicate, not much above a whisper, "Make damn good and sure you love her. Or you'll both be fucked."

The first bright drop of shine slipped out the end of the copper piping, pinging into the waiting pitcher.

Lori didn't visit him the next day or the next. Jackson could have just let it go. Most things will go away if you ignore them. His father had always said that, but his mom would always slam or bang something and proclaim that was *not* true of the bills. The following morning he looked up Lori's father's number in the phone book, dialled, and asked to speak to Lori. He waited a minute then heard the receiver being passed over with a whisper, "It's a man."

Lori answered with a question. "Hello?"

"Hi."

"Jackson!" She remembered the little smile he had given her before she left, the beers he poured for her, the wood carvings, the weight of his body on hers.

"How are you?" He had reminded himself to ask this, practised it.

"Good, Jackson. I'm really good. Gee, I don't think you've ever called here before. This is great. I was just doing my toenails. Geeky, eh? It's that really bright red shade I had on a couple of weeks ago. Wild. I was going out later, just to the store, I mean. You're lucky you caught me. How are you?"

"Okay."

Then Jackson wasn't sure exactly what was the polite way to ask a girl if she was pregnant. "I was wondering, cause you said you wanted to get married, I just wondered, if you were pregnant or anything."

Then it was Lori's turn to pause. He didn't care about her, he was only interested in himself. He cared enough to call, to ask her. He didn't just walk off like lots of them did. He wasn't interested in her for herself. He would only marry her if he had to. He would marry her if she was pregnant. If she was pregnant she could make a scene and he would comfort her and propose and they would fix up the cabin and he would hook up the toilet and build on another room or maybe two. She'd be out of this shit-hole and have a home of her own and a baby and Jackson looking after them all. And after the baby came he'd give up drinking, well not completely, but he'd move the bootlegging out into a shed or something and only drink on weekends, which wouldn't be bad. If she were pregnant. And she could *say* she was. And by the time he found out she probably *would* be and they'd laugh about it.

"Uh. No. I'm not pregnant. Or anything."

"Well. That's great then."

"Yeah. Thank god, eh?"

"Yeah."

Lori waited, wondering if he was going to ask her to come over. Since he was happy. Since she wasn't pregnant.

Jackson didn't have anything to go on. He tried to remember the lines they used on the soaps. ". . . 'cause I'm not ahh, really ready, you know, for uhmm, a relationship right now . . . ?"

There was silence.

"You're not mad, are you?" he asked.

"No."

"Okay then."

Lori was going to say goodbye but the receiver was already buzzing in her ear. Twenty-two years old she was. Twenty-two. She cradled the receiver in her lap. She didn't have the strength to hang up.

Matthew and Jackson recovered from the first batch of shine just as the experimental potato mash was ready for the still. Jackson set up the machine and they sat back in their chairs, watching droplets form on the cooling pipe that poked above the water in the sink. Jackson felt a shrug of feeling in his chest, a kind of gurgle bubbling up through the beer. It was strange, and frightening after all this time. His brother, Matthew, had helped him out. Not that he'd said anything that great, just that he'd said something. He had heard his brother's voice. For a second he thought he might reach over and touch him. He swallowed. The bubble was almost painful. Matthew, he thought, thank you.

"Matthew," he said. The word pierced the air between them, stark naked. He cringed at the intimacy of it. He felt a bit dizzy and had to gulp a breath. Matthew was looking at him. "This is going to be a great batch," Jackson said.

LARRY LYNCH

The Sitter

"**O**kay?" Cami's father stood in the doorway of her room. She rolled over on her bed to face the wall. "Is it the babysitter? I've arranged for a new one," he said. Cami lay still – an opossum. "Is it school?" he asked. She didn't answer. "Cami?"

"It's everything," she said to the wall.

It was moving. It was leaving her friends. It was her father's stupid career. It was having to tell people, tell them all over again, that it was only the two of them, Cami and her father.

Her full name, Camilla, was her mother's legacy to her. That, and the burden of trying to explain being motherless everywhere they went. It was easier to say divorce or plane crash than to tell people what her father had told her: "She was young, Cami. And you were so little. She found being a mother harder than anything in the world." Her father's explanation would be unbelievable to others. She thought it seemed unbelievable to him.

One day in that late, reluctant spring, her first day at another new school, Cami's fifth-grade teacher introduced her. "Class, this is Camilla," she announced to snickers. "It's Cami," Cami corrected, but the horrid utterance had already begun to circulate like a fart in church, and it swirled above her head. She felt like an oddity; an odd, one-parented girl in a land of judgmental, perfect pre-teens.

He sat on her bed and rubbed the back of her neck. She liked it, resented it, wished she was older, wished he would leave her alone, wished she could lie in bed with him like she did when she was younger. "It's going to be all right," he said, "give it some time." Her father smelled good, like the cologne sample pages in magazines. She could not stay mad at him. Her large orange cat lounged in a puddle of light near the window. It stretched as if to invite her to rub its belly, but she knew it would scratch her if she did.

"There's someone new coming over tomorrow after school." He stroked her hair and she lay still, facing the wall. "I'm leaving work early to pick you up so we can meet her when she gets here. Okay?" She didn't answer. "Okay?" he said into the back of her neck, leaning on her and tickling her ribs. She squirmed and rolled over to face him, and as hard as she tried, she could not keep from smiling. "Good," he said.

"Can I stay after school by myself when I'm thirteen?" she called as he left.

"We'll see," he answered.

"Fourteen?"

"We'll see."

Every babysitter Cami's father hired was met with Cami's disapproval. She hated them, she told him. They smoked, they stank, they talked on the phone for hours, they snooped through the house; she could be very convincing. When the new babysitter arrived, Cami did not have to roll her eyes, pinch her nose, stick her finger down her throat, or do any of the other things that brought that panicked look to her father's face; it happened instantly when he opened the door. He stood there, looking nervous and incompetent while the new girl stared down at him. Perhaps it was because she was taller. Perhaps it was the shirt she wore that exposed the gold hoop that pierced her belly button. Perhaps it was her wide, wide pant legs or the psychedelic, crocheted bag that hung over her shoulder. The new girl smiled broadly, friendly, and Cami's father stuck out his hand.

"You're Kate," he said. Not a question, or an exclamation, but more a bewildered statement, the way one might react if they caught their grandmother smoking pot. The face did not match the name.

"That's me," she said and turned to Cami.

"That's Cami," her father said.

"Cool name." Kate nodded in approval at them both.

Cami saw her father relax after being congratulated for her cool name. She knew he would be going back to work, leaving her with the seventies girl, and reasons why she would hate her were already congealing in her mind.

"Okay," he said, like he was about to divulge a big secret, "I'm leaving." He scanned their faces for comprehension. "Any problems, my number is on the fridge." This was standard; the number hung there under a banana-shaped magnet as it did for all the other babysitters. "Gotta go." He leaned down and kissed Cami, who was rigid, unreciprocating.

As was her practice, she went directly to her room. She said she was going to do homework, which she hoped would be understood as "Don't bother me." Normally, she would lie on her bed, doodling in her textbooks, listening to the noise of the TV coming from the living room, and the cupboard doors opening and closing in the kitchen. Cami felt babysitters had an innate ability to find potato chips in any house and always helped themselves. Having someone strange in her house, watching her TV, eating her chips, talking on her phone, and ignoring her just like she wanted – these things bothered her. She was thankful it was only for a few hours after school, and that her father felt guilty enough about it not to venture far in the evenings or on the weekends without her.

When Cami and her father watched television at night, he sat on the couch and she would sometimes sit on the floor with her back resting against his legs. He flipped through catalogues and asked her which curtains matched which bedspreads and held the catalogue in front of her face, blocking her view of the TV. The furniture they moved from their apartment to their new house looked miniature in the larger rooms. "I don't know," she would say and change channels indiscriminately. Sometimes she would catch him staring at her, then say to him: "What?" "Nothing," would be his surprised answer, snapping from his gaze, "just looking at a monkey," and he'd chase her with his tickle-ready fingers. Sometimes he just sat there looking defeated and lonely. In those instances, Cami could say or do nothing that would help; for if she could she would have done so for herself.

When he was not home she took the catalogues to her room. Not to look at the furniture and drapes and towels that her father struggled to choose, but at the women, deciding which were the prettiest, which, if any, looked like her or had her round cheeks and wide, dark eyes.

"Are you hungry?" Kate said and came into Cami's room. Cami sat up. "No," she said, emphatic, and scrutinized Kate as she wandered about the room like she was at Wal-Mart, looking at and touching Cami's things. Kate's hair hung straight down her back. She parted it somewhat in the middle and kept sweeping errant strands behind her ears. Her ears were pierced in several places and earrings hung around them like seats on a Ferris wheel. They dangled hypnotically.

Cami could see that her No had not registered. Kate moved over to her bureau and picked up a magazine. "You like these guys?" she asked and turned the picture of the band on the cover in Cami's direction. They were Cami's favourite. "They're okay," Cami said.

Kate put the magazine back and surveyed the room. "Where's your mom?" she asked. "Working too?"

If Cami had been a cat, she would have scratched Kate; she would have run up her leg and clawed her belly, and maybe hooked a claw into that ring in her belly button. Cami's eyes narrowed to slits and her lips went thin and pale. But, as she always did when she was asked, she said, "It's only my dad and me."

"That's cool," Kate said, looking neither surprised nor sympathetic. Everything was cool. Cami was hating cool. Kate sat on the bed, and Cami pulled her knees into her chest. "So, what do you want to do?" Kate asked her.

Cami shrugged and inched back toward the wall, bracing her knees with her arms.

"Do you want to listen to some music? Do you have any CDs?"

"A few," Cami said reluctantly, "in the living room."

Her cat arched against the wall near the door. Cami watched Kate pick it up on her way out of the room. "What's her name?" she asked.

"It's Tiger, and it's a *he*," she snapped. "He'll scratch you," she said, more hopeful than cautionary, and watched Kate hold up the surprised cat under the front legs like a baby, rubbing noses with it. "Pretty Tiger," Kate cooed, then tucked the cat under her arm and rubbed its head. The cat's tail flicked wildly against her exposed lower back as she carried it down the hall.

Babysitters should eat chips, lie on the couch, talk on the phone, and not bug her. That is what they should do, Cami thought. Not come into her room, ask a bunch of nosy questions, and pick up her cat. And why did she have so many earrings? Two were not enough? Four? Cami thought about how many times she'd asked her father to allow her to get her ears pierced. "Someday," he would say, not really trying to put her off, she thought, just not knowing that it was important to her – a girl thing, a growing-up thing. He frowned when they went shopping, and smiled helplessly at the clerks as Cami coaxed and pleaded to buy her what she wanted – not the cute sweaters with the animals or cartoon characters, but clothes like other girls wore, like the ones in her school, the girls with earrings, who talked to boys, the ones who turned and giggled when "Camilla" spread through the room like a gas.

And like a strange, noxious gas itself, music spread from down the hall into her room. Not one of her CDs, something new. Cami went to see what her new and nonconforming babysitter was doing.

"Your dad has some really old ones here," Kate said as she pulsed in front of the record player, holding an album up for Cami to see. The cover had three men with long, womanish hair and neatly cut beards. The Bee Gees. Tiger stood in the middle of the room looking defensive.

"I didn't know that worked," Cami said of the record player. Kate's shoulders dipped with the music, her hips moved back and forth, and Cami watched the ring wriggle as her belly button puckered and winked to the rhythm. Kate's head bobbed as she read the album cover.

Cami moved closer to see exactly how many records her father had. She knelt and pulled some from the drawer below the turntable. They were light and flimsy with faded pictures of strange-looking groups on the front. She was kneeling close to Kate and watching her pant legs billow and her painted toes tap on the floor. She smelled faintly of cigarette smoke, and of fruit. It was her hair, Cami thought. Apples.

"Do you smoke?" Cami asked. Kate said "No" and Cami stared at her in disbelief.

The records were of little curiosity to Cami; only their number and that they were probably older than she was. She stuffed them back into their slots. When she stood, she was looking directly into Kate's skewered navel. Kate caught her staring.

"Do you like it?" Kate asked, flipping the ring up and down with a casual finger.

She did not know what to say, and remembered the time she saw a woman breast-feeding on a bench at the mall, and how she had stared, though she really did not want to. "Did it hurt?" she asked.

"A little." Kate answered. She smiled and put on another record.

"Does it come out?"

"Yeah," she said, "do you want to see?"

Cami shook her head to say no, but "Yes" came from her mouth.

Kate undid the clasp and slid the ring from the tiny holes in her navel. The little wounds looked neither sore nor grotesque, as Cami had expected. Kate slid the ring back in with ease; first in one tiny hole, then out the other, then fastened it. "See?" she said.

Kate played records and cooked some fries and fish sticks in the oven – her specialty, she joked. Cami followed her in and out of the kitchen and living room, keeping her distance, acting nonchalant, and stifling the questions that filled her mind. She sat on the couch eating (she was hungry after all) and watched Kate reel to the music, alive in it. The couch felt new and the room felt different. In the waning light of the afternoon, in the odd scratchy beat of another era, being that close to a babysitter for that long, it felt like a different house.

Her father looked too surprised to smile when she told him that things went okay. "So it's okay that she comes back?" he asked. Cami shrugged. She brushed her teeth while her father leaned against the bathroom door, staring at her with his glassed-over gaze.

Toothpaste frothed down her chin. "She was playing your records," she said, expecting it might be a bad thing. The records were obviously something sacred; he had carted them halfway across the country, but never listened to them. "And I think she smokes." Her habitual resentment resurfaced.

"My records?" he said, wiping her face with a towel. "Did you like them?"

"No. They were weird." This was his punishment for not being upset with Kate.

He kissed her on the forehead and swept her hair back when she got into bed. She could see his face soften. And as she lay there for a long time, unable to fall asleep, she pinched her belly button, then her earlobes, as hard as she could to see how much it hurt. She heard scratchy music coming from the living room, records and a life she never knew her father had. She fell asleep trying to picture her father when his records were new, when he was younger, happier, dancing to that music, holding a woman and whispering into her round cheeks.

In the morning she asked again.

"No."

"Please?"

"Cami . . ."

"Please?"

"No."

"Why not?"

"You're too young."

"But . . ."

"Cami."

"Please."

"No."

"Please, please, please, please, please, please, please, please, please, please, please."

"Cami, you don't need your ears pierced. Wait till you're older."

"When will that be?"

"Soon."

In the heat of the spring sun, tulips that had kept themselves secret under the snow since Cami and her father moved east pressed through the warming soil and basked next to the front of their house. In the nurturing rain and the warmth of the season, things grew. Cami's curiosity grew.

How old are you? Does your father let you stay out late? How late? Do you keep a diary? I think I will keep a diary. Do you have a lot of friends? What are their names? Are they all seventeen too? Do you like school? How old were you when you started wearing a bra? I think I should get one. My dad gets weird when I ask him. Do you have a phone in your room? Really? Cool! Do you think I should let my hair grow? When people kiss on TV are they doing it for real? I think it would be cool to be on TV. Do you? Yeah. Cool.

Cami told her father: "Kate knows lots of stuff."

"I bet she does," he said.

"She said she was nine when she got her ears pierced."

"Really?"

"Yeah. And she says that people on TV really are kissing, but they don't mean it. And she said she was ten when she got a bra. Do you think I should get one?"

"I don't know. Isn't it almost time for bed?"

"Don't you think Kate is cool?"

"Cool?"

"Yeah. She said she would take me to get my ears pierced if you said it was okay. So, can I?"

"Cami..."

"Please?" She said it only once.

"We'll see."

"Great," she squealed and scampered to her room, picking up the cat in the hall before it had time to get away.

Cami was not nervous. She trusted Kate and felt it was mutual, because she promised not to tell her father that they'd spent the money he had given them on a bra, and not ear piercing. Cami held the tiny blue box in her hand as she twisted in front of the mirror to see if the outline of her new bra showed through each and every shirt she owned. She held the little gold studs up to her ears to see how they looked – studs Kate had given her, ones Kate had worn when she was ten. Cami was not nervous. She reassured herself aloud. She trusted Kate. Not nervous at all. Kate promised that it would not hurt much. Kate said she had pierced her own, once. Cami pinched her lobes. "I'm almost ready," she could hear Kate call from the kitchen. She pinched them harder and her fingernails left her earlobes red, with crescent-shaped indentations. Her cat was nowhere to be seen.

"Are you sure you want me to do this?" Kate appeared in the doorway of Cami's room and caught her by surprise. Cami was wearing the tie-dyed shirt Kate had made for her. She turned in the mirror, examining her newly accentuated physique. "You can hardly see it," Kate said and grinned.

"Really?" Cami said. She was disappointed.

"Things are ready," Kate said. "Why are your ears so red?"

"Uhm . . . because . . . this isn't going to hurt, right? You said it wouldn't." Cami covered her ears.

"I said it will a little," Kate said. "You don't have to do it."

"I want to. Will it bleed?"

"A little. Are you sure?"

Cami nodded.

"And you'll have to take care of them so they don't get infected."

Cami nodded again.

Water boiled in a pot on the stove, rubbing alcohol and a bar of soap waited on the counter. Cami sat on a stool near the sink. Kate took the earrings from the box and put them in the boiling water along with a pin she took from her bag. She gave Cami two ice cubes and told her to squeeze her earlobe between them. Cami did. The ice melted and water ran down her arm. She watched Kate intensely and began to sweat and itch in her new bra. The ice burned her fingers and ear, and she was sure it was going to be painful.

"Keep holding it," Kate said and fished the needle and earrings out of the pot with a spoon, then doused them with the alcohol. Kate took the ice cubes from Cami and swabbed her ear with the alcohol. She held a bar of soap behind Cami's ear and stretched the lobe over it, holding it in place with her thumb. "Hold still," was all the warning she gave before Cami felt the pinch of the needle and the little gold stud sliding into place.

"Go and have a look," Kate said. Cami scampered to the bathroom mirror. She lightly touched the stud, and waggled her earlobe with her finger, impressed at her own durability and pluck. A speck of blood formed behind the gold but did not perturb her. She ran back to the kitchen where Kate returned the needle to the boiling water.

"It looks good, doesn't it?" She pulled back her hair and cocked her head.

"Very nice," Kate said, "now let's do the other one."

"It did hurt some," Cami said, "but not too bad." Her face glowed. "You're good at this."

"Thanks. You did great, too. Hold these," and she pressed ice to Cami's other ear.

It was like Christmas, and Kate was like Santa. Cami was getting exactly what she wanted and she could not wait for her father to get home. She did not mind the cold water dripping down her arm.

The phone rang. "Tell Dad that I can't come to the phone. Tell him I'm doing homework. No. Tell him I'm in the bathroom." Water pooled on the floor.

Kate answered. "Hello . . . Oh, hi. . . . Not much. Piercing Cami's ears. . . . Yes, really. . . ." Cami's face plummeted. "I'll ask her. . . . Okay. . . . Tomorrow. . . . Okay. I'm sure he won't mind. He seems really nice. . . . Okay. Me too. . . . Bye."

"Why did you tell him?" Cami accused. "I thought –"

"That was Derek, not your father."

"Who's Derek?"

"My boyfriend. Are you ready?"

Boyfriend, Cami thought. Kate took the ice from her ears.

Cami had questions to ask. How old is he? What does he look like? How long had they been dating? Does he call her all the time? Why hadn't she mentioned him before? "Ouch!" And with the prick of the pin the questions stopped swirling and her ears had matching holes.

Cami went from the mirror in her room, to the mirror in her father's bedroom, back and forth, twisting and changing clothes, studying her ears and her bra, and how it all looked together, while Kate put everything away. Cami sat on the couch and tried to think of something more mature to talk about with Kate; after all, they did have things in common now. Two, anyway – or four, depending how you counted. But Kate was practising lines for a play and was not chatty. Cami paced and modelled and fidgeted and touched her ears until her father came home. When he arrived, she pranced before him, holding her hair back and turning her head from side to side, showing him both shining studs with a speck of dried blood behind each.

"They're beautiful," he said. "Very mature." He looked relieved.

"And . . ." Cami said, twisting on the balls of her feet and thrusting out her chest.

"And what?"

When Cami turned her back (hoping her bra was more noticeable from that side) Kate plucked at her own strap for him to notice and mouthed the word "bra."

His relieved look deserted him. "Oh, yes . . . a new . . . ah, a bra. . . . It's very . . . ah . . . new."

The end of the school year drew nearer and the sun stayed longer each night after supper and etched long shadows across the lawn. The tulips withered next to the house. The cat slept in the picture window, absorbing the sun in its orange fur. Cami's ears were almost completely healed. Kate studied a lot and rehearsed lines for her play. Derek watched wrestling on TV.

Derek was cool, too, Cami thought, or at least he acted that way in spite of the pimples on his forehead and cheeks. He would arrive at the house after school, and although Cami's father had given unenthusiastic consent, Derek always left before Cami's father got home from work. Cami liked the flag Derek had sewn over a hole in the seat of his ripped jeans. And she was beginning to consider his very faint moustache not as hilarious as the first time she'd seen it. The first thing Kate did was advise him not to smoke in the house.

His first day there, Cami walked into the room and they separated quickly and Kate's face turned crimson.

"Were you guys kissing?" Cami asked, trying to act like she had seen it all before and that nothing surprised her.

"I was just smelling her hair," Derek said and grinned foolishly.

"Yeah, right," Cami said and tilted her head, giving him her how-dumb-do-you-think-I-am look. "Kiss her all you want. I don't care." She tried to act indifferent, but was never far from them while he was there.

She felt older just being around them, a witness to the intricacies of courtship. Kate laughed differently at the things Derek did and said; different from the way she laughed at Cami. When she laughed at Derek she would lean into him and he would put a casual arm around her shoulders or a hand on her bare lower back. Cami thought that was why he tried to be humorous more often, especially if Kate was standing close to him. Cami noticed that Kate sat sideways on the couch to study, and tucked her feet under Derek's legs as he watched TV, as if her painted toes were cold. To Cami, that closeness seemed effortless and natural and a lifetime away.

"Are you going to get married someday and have kids?" she asked them one night.

Derek never looked from the TV. "Not if she's going to college, we're not."

That night at supper, Derek took a beer from the fridge and drank it. Kate got mad. Pretty mad, Cami guessed, because Kate sat on the floor while Derek sulked on the couch.

After that, out of allegiance, there was something Cami found not so likeable about Derek. Kate's knitted eyebrows and pursed lips confirmed it. There was something ugly about his ripening pimples, something repulsive and dirty about the way he flicked ashes on the front step. There was something extremely annoying about the way he monopolized the remote control.

Cami broke the silence. "Is that all you like? Stupid wrestling?"

He did not respond immediately. He was sitting there, Cami thought, trying to come up with something funny to say; something stupid to make Kate laugh and make her want to sit next to him.

"What? You don't like the Hulkster?" he said as he jumped up and put a wriggling Cami in a pretend headlock. His belt buckle hooked her earring. When she tried to pull away, it felt as though the gold stud had ripped her ear off. Cami screamed and clutched the side of her head. Derek froze.

Kate rushed to her side, and knelt and took her head in her hands. Cami could smell her apples and ink. Kate's hands were smooth and gentle as she turned her head to inspect the damage. "It's okay, Cami. It's not ripped. It's okay."

"Hey. It was an accident," he said. "Don't be such a baby."

"Derek. You're an asshole." Kate's face was hard.

Cami's ear throbbed and her confusion swelled. She did not want to cry in front of them, to be a baby. She wanted to run to her room and cry into her pillow, to muffle her sobs and absorb her tears. She wanted to run over and kick Derek in the shins, and throw her hissing cat in his face. She wanted Kate to let go of her arm so she could run from them to her room. She wanted Kate to use both arms to hold her, tightly, and not let her go. Cami stood there, wincing as she touched her bleeding ear with fingers covered in her salty tears.

Derek left.

With her thumb, Kate swept a tear from Cami's cheek. "Are you okay?" Cami nodded and sniffed. Kate smiled, and in her soft, even voice said, "With eyes so brown, I was expecting brown tears." She showed Cami her shining thumb.

How far away is college? Will you come home on weekends? Are you still going to go out with Derek? Will there be a phone in your room there? How much does it cost to send a letter? Can you come home for my birthday? Cami wanted to know all these things and more, but did not ask. And she thought she had finished crying, until Kate hugged her and she started again – woeful sobs, and plump, streaming tears. Kate's earrings jingled in Cami's ear like chimes in a summer's apple-scented breeze.

When the curtain came down on Kate, the audience applauded the resurrected unicorn and her chorus of bowing animals. Cami and her father rushed home; Kate was coming from the play to their house to babysit, and Cami wanted to make a card for her before she got there. Cami could still hear the applause as she and her father hurried across the parking lot to their car. They passed Derek. He was leaning against the auditorium, the glowing ember of his cigarette casting an orange light into his squinting and evasive eyes.

On a piece of coloured paper she drew a unicorn: Kate the Unicorn. She drew the white and blue ribbons that curled into Kate's hair and floated and danced in the air when she leapt around the stage. She drew the flowing white dress Kate wore, and showed its silky layers fluttering behind a prancing and carefree unicorn. She drew the glittering spiral horn that grew from her head, and she drew the audience in front of the stage that stood and applauded the star. She drew herself, applauding among the appreciative, stating proudly to the stranger beside her that the unicorn, the star, was *her* babysitter.

When Kate arrived, Cami was already in her pyjamas with the card in her hand. She was hyper and spewed questions. Were you nervous? Did you see me clapping? Did you sign any autographs? Can I stay up late? There's no school tomorrow. We can make popcorn. Did you save the horn?

Kate was still in her costume; glittering makeup sparkled blue and gold across her cheeks. Her horn was missing and she soberly held her bag over her shoulder. Her smile was bright, but brief, when Cami gave her the card. "The Best Babysitter."

Cami's father wrote down a number where he could be reached before he left. Kate made popcorn and they sat on the couch watching the news. Kate hadn't changed from her flowing white dress and the blue and white ribbons entwined in her hair hung over her shoulder. She answered Cami's questions with little enthusiasm until eventually Cami struggled to stay awake.

"When are you leaving for college?" Cami asked, leaning her head on Kate's shoulder, preparing to close her eyes. Next month, was Kate's answer. To that, Cami said only, "Oh." Her cat rubbed itself across Kate's legs, then jumped up and curled by the armrest, purring.

Kate placed a pillow on her lap. Cami laid her head there and looked up, fading from consciousness. The blue and gold sparkles on Kate's cheeks glittered like the heavens, and her earrings hung like planets in the tails of the shooting stars that were the ribbons in her hair. Cami's limp body twitched occasionally in opposition to sleep, but eventually her mouth fell open, drawing peaceful breaths, and her hand hung limp over the side of the couch.

She started to dream – a dream of a unicorn surrounded by children with their outstretched arms. There were flowers and the smell of apples and a faint, unsettling odour of smoke. Fingers ran through her hair. "Do me a favour," she heard, and her body lunged to a half-sleep. "Don't ever go with a guy who will make you choose." And sparkles of blue and gold on streams of mascara ran down to the corners of a trembling mouth. There were many children, and cats chasing balls. The unicorn smiled and whirled, trying to touch all the outstretched hands, but kept missing Cami's. The whirling and spinning obscured the unicorn's face. "Look at me," Cami tried to shout above the others. Then she felt herself being carried on a scent and in arms so familiar that she nestled into them, comforted, secure, until she was set down and she awoke. Her father kissed her on the forehead, then turned to leave her room.

"Dad," she said in a fragile voice.

"Yes, Cami."

"Where is Kate?"

"She went home."

"Oh," she said, under the weight of realizing where she was and that she had been dreaming.

"She's going to college," she blurted out. That part wasn't a dream.

"I know. She told me."

"Can I sleep in your bed?" she asked and held out her arms so she could be lifted and carried.

She felt half her age, clinging to his neck as he carried her down the hall, and she wondered how long it took to dream a dream.

"Dad?" she asked.

"Yes, Cami?"

"Before she goes, I should tell her I'll miss her."

He laid her in bed, covered her and brushed her hair back as he always did. "I bet she already knows," he said. "But you should tell her just the same."

SANDRA SABATINI

The One With the News

Ambrose came back from the dead last night. Worm-eaten, stinking of compost gone awry. He was happy to see me and to be back in his right mind with Peggy. She kept picking up grey bits of flesh from the carpet, shaking her head at his untidiness, yet delighted nevertheless to have him home. I knew that days were passing in my dream, and as they did, he began to look better. The flesh adhered more specifically to his face; I couldn't see so much of his gums when he smiled. He seemed to grow lips during dinner. At the soup course, I distinctly heard his teeth clacking together, but by the time he was eating the hazelnut torte, I could hear smacking noises. I also knew that he got better because I was there.

The dream made me wish I had a therapist. I told Larry about it in the morning, and I asked him if he'd ever seen a body coming out of a grave instead of going into one. He supervises the burial crew at Woodlawn but he's also in charge of exhumations. He gave me a kiss and said, "Forget it, Connie, you're scary enough." He didn't want to give me any details. I didn't need them.

I have a scar on my knee from falling on the sidewalk in front of Wendy's house when we were six years old. We played What Time Is It Mr. Wolf, and I turned, screaming, to run away from Kevin McPhee, who was the wolf. I tripped on the same heaved-up concrete that made me fall off my bike the week before. I had just lost the scab and there I was, bleeding and crying. The object of my friend's disgust. I don't remember Wendy ever falling. My father heard me and came to take me home. He put another Band-Aid on my knee and read to me about Nubbins the farm horse who had a pretty good life.

This was before my father died. I remember the press of the cold kitchen table against my thighs. It seemed strange and thrilling that it was my father peeling back the bandage and gently pressing it to my skin, and not my mother. I didn't know he would be able to do such a thing at all, let alone with great gentleness. He didn't live much longer after that. As though God decided that this one act should be enough to last me until Ambrose came along.

When I was ten years old my mother bought a three-bedroom cottage on the Deer River in the Kawarthas. I think it was the Kawarthas. I used to listen to the weather reports for the Haliburtons, the Muskokas, and the Kawarthas. "Which are we?" I asked my brother. He was fishing and didn't care.

The cottage stood three feet off the ground on concrete blocks. The bedroom doorways were covered by curtains that didn't extend across the whole opening, and that fell down in the slightest breeze. It was an uncomfortable place, and dirty. There was no beach at the edge of the river where we swam, only a muddy embankment, and none of us cared to clean our feet before we went back to the cottage to change.

The outhouse, slapped together with slabs of splintering pine, had to be moved every few years. Dark and pungent with lime and shit, it at least had a door that locked, so sometimes I went there to change into my bathing suit, away from view, holding my breath.

There wasn't a good season at the cottage. It wasn't insulated so there was no question of going there in the winter, and sometimes the roof collapsed in the early spring when the weight of the melting snow forced its way through rotting beams. One year we went to open the cottage and found the furniture wet and the coffee table bowed like a smile in the middle. The wood was warped and never did break, but ever after it was useless as a place to rest a mug of coffee. My brother has it still in his family room. It is a good conversation piece.

Spring meant black flies; summer meant mosquitoes and my cousins.

My cousins were dangerous people. They drank and smoked cigarettes and hashish while their parents sat in the cottage, somehow believing that we were all playing Monopoly. They fed frogs to snakes and then put firecrackers in the snakes' mouths. This was the only habit they tried to keep from their parents. I, who loved telling, never told. I sat still at the edge of the circle of sand so as not to be splattered with exploding snake and frog guts.

Anything dreary or dingy or embarrassing that can happen to a young girl happened to me at that cottage. I fell into the river on the long weekend in May and nearly drowned before I was pulled out by the man who rented a room in my mother's house, the man I had grown up hating. Afterwards I sat in my brother's room, shaking, topless, a towel around my shoulders and no one's arm, listening to my aunt scold me again about safety rules and the proper way to get into a boat. Menstruation began, of course, at the cottage, and I was left to deal with it in the outhouse, left to deal with the stomach pain in my doorless bedroom, quietly dreaming of blood.

I was sure there must be a quiet place somewhere, where my elbows wouldn't knock the bedside table, with a large window and a cold sea and a beach, chilled and clammy, that would make the bones of my feet ache. My mother said bare feet would make my period cramps bad, but I didn't believe they could get worse. That was before I found out that life offers unlimited opportunity for getting worse.

I read all of Ian Fleming in my room. Would I be the sort of girl James Bond would fall in love with? Was there any question? My mother played cards in the kitchen with her sister and my uncle and the other man. Euchre was the game of choice. Before I could do long division, I knew what was trump and how to take tricks and go alone. They were all very fat people who could barely sit comfortably at a table. They smoked thousands of cigarettes. My aunt had orange hair, and a partial plate. Her legs were mapped in red and turquoise veins below her Bermuda shorts. Her bifocals were connected by a silver chain around her wattled turkey neck. She favoured my brother who was friendly to her and fetched her lighter. She didn't hit me but she had a slicing tongue. I thought her meanness must have something to do with the strange wiry bits of metal she had around some of her teeth. I was grown up with children of my own before I understood that the metal kept her false teeth in place and gave her sibilants a sharpness that seemed to flay me.

My uncle was bald but he had hair everywhere else on his body. He went whole summers without wearing a shirt. He taught me to play the guitar and to swim and to tuck in all of my shirts. He never said anything when he tried to slip his hands onto my rib cage and up. I never said anything and I didn't stay away either. I thought it might have been an accident and didn't believe it was and I wondered if it might happen again.

I thought that all men matured into a strange shape, alien to the one they grew up with. Up until about their mid-twenties most of the men I knew seemed normal. Slim of hip, more or less broad of shoulder. Delightfully constructed of clean, straight lines. Then something happened. My uncle, for instance, and the man who lived with us looked okay from behind but when they turned sideways it was clear that years of determined drinking had altered their shadows forever. Sideways they were gravid with the beer that gave them huge bellies and C-cup breasts. The disproportion between hips, shoulders, legs, arms, and these huge stomachs made them seem like Martians, candidates for *Unsolved Mysteries*. How did it happen? What was in there? They stroked the greying hairs, caressed their bellies, even named them.

My mother was at the cottage, smoking. She sat beside the man who lived with us and who sometimes kissed her. He was not my friend, though he tried to be. I could never like him or pray for him, even when it was pointed out to me that doing so would make Jesus happy.

A one-eyed taxidermist lived down the road from our cottage in a long, low bungalow set well back from the gravel road. The property was surrounded by a mesh fence topped with barbed wire. We believed the fence to be electric and never touched it. If we stood at the gate and waited in the blasting sun among angry deer flies, eventually the doctor, as we called him, would come out and make his slow way down the driveway, preceded by his dog, Laddie. The doctor told us that Laddie, who had one blue eye and one almost pure white eye, was part wolf and part husky. We knew by the way he looked at us that he would eat us if he got the chance; we didn't pet Laddie. We followed the doctor up to the house and shivered in the dark garage waiting for the door to open on a house of wonders. The doctor was an artist with the carcasses of bears, wolves, cougars, fish, owls, butter-flies, weasels, rats, and snakes. His favourite display was of Laddie the First, a beagle who'd had, it seemed, a much friend-lier outlook on life. Our favourite display was at the very end of the room: an illuminated glass cabinet, faintly smelling of formaldehyde, housed the three-headed baby pig that had died at birth and had been donated to the doctor by one of the local farmers. It was small, grotesque, irresistible, with three sets of limpid eyes and three damp-looking snouts, preserved, warm, needy. We couldn't pull ourselves from the pinkness of it.

We whispered in its presence, *Could this happen to a person?*
Sure, my brother said, *I've seen it.*
Have not.
Have too.
Stupid.
You're the one who's stupid.
Am not.
Are too.
Haven't you ever heard of thalidomide?
No.
Stupid.
Stupid.
You could have been a thalidomide baby.
What's that?
I'm not telling. Ask Mom.
He always knew everything before me.

One night I had to give up my room to a friend of my uncle's. I slept on the springs of the old couch in the living room listening to the fist fight outside the front door. My uncle and the man, two fat and ancient men, were fighting over my mother who matched them pound for pound and year for year. It made my stomach cold to listen. Who were these people and why did they drink so much and if they had to drink so much beer, why not wait and let it knock them down instead of each other? Being drunk did not help them. They sounded like my brother and me only stupider, slower.

You're a lousy son of a bitch.

YOU'RE A LOUSY SON OF A BITCH!

AM NOT!

ARE TOO!

Followed by punches and vomiting. My mother stayed in her room and seemed to be asleep on another planet. I followed her example. In the morning I poked my head into my room to get my shoes. My uncle's friend was lying on top of my bed, naked with a purple sausage on his belly. My head was back in the living room before I realized what it was I might have seen.

I thought it would be good to get away from this life. We grew up on Cinderella, but my cousins all seemed to know that she could have nothing to do with them. Woolworth's and the Five and Dime were supposed to have everything we needed. We were all supposed to have been born with a love for the green and blue swans on the tops of our console TVs.

The people up the hill from our cottage lived in their place all year-round. Bill had brought Lucia over from Italy after the war, but he never actually married her in spite of giving her four or five children, not counting the two from Bill's marriage to Brenda. Lucia had straight black hair which she cut bluntly at her jaw with her kitchen scissors and wore parted in the middle. Her eyes were blue but one of them didn't move. I could never tell, when I visited, if she was yelling at me or one of Bill's kids. She spoke with a lisp from having been born without upper teeth. She had false ones but they were uncomfortable, especially when clean; she preferred to do without.

Their house was unfinished: exposed, pink insulation

between studs, a screwed-down plywood floor. The kitchen's exterior walls were made of gyprock, but between the rooms were only bare two-by-fours through which we could see the wiring and dust at the back of the stove. Lucia was strong. She fed and stroked the rabbits in the shed that were kept until the weather was nice enough to start the Hibachi. It was the sort of house where the pet bitch could give birth to a litter of puppies in the dirt basement and live undetected for weeks while we cuddled them. Until Bill finally found out and shot them with his .22, finishing off an afternoon of Labatt's. Lucia cleaned up the mess.

I see her now in the Health Centre, sometimes at the same table as Ambrose. I can't say hello. I'm sure she doesn't recognize me, even if it's me she's looking at. It doesn't surprise me that she's somehow lost her mind, but it makes me nervous, seeing her with Ambrose whose ears are kind of big and whose front teeth, if he's thirsty, protrude a little. I don't want Lucia mistaking him for a rabbit.

I went hunting for bullfrogs with my brother in the marshes around our cottage. He expected me to take the oar and cosh the frog over the head and toss it into the boat. I won his approval through bloodthirstiness. When the front of the boat was full we headed back to the cottage to chop off the legs and feet and then we would peel back the skin as if it were a silk stocking. Our mother wouldn't cook them; she said the legs were still alive and would be jumping in the hot butter. We fried them ourselves, adding salt and pepper, and ate them out of the pan on the cottage porch, burning our fingertips. We decimated the frog population in that region north of Peterborough. We stopped their voices and ate their legs, so the wiser ones moved away. The last few years at the cottage we were reduced to eating chicken legs, which are not as sweet as fresh frog. My children don't know that I was a ravager of wetlands; they think I've always been a responsible composter and recycler. They are gentle children whose uncles keep their hands to themselves while watching Disney movies, and whose eyes dampen when the cat goes over the waterfall, even though they know it lives.

My brother doesn't kill frogs any more and has gone on to live a life I no longer admire, even as he does not admire mine. We used to kill together but we aren't close now. The carcasses of hundreds of frogs are not between us, but something is. It could be our mother who died with her legs still covered in skin and attached to her body, uncooked, uneaten, but no less devoured.

I sat beside my mother's hospital bed, swallowing the familiar odour of formaldehyde and decay. Her flesh was disturbingly pink. Her eyes were glassy with pain or with medication or with a vision of another world. I thought, she's free of the man now. Maybe I am too. I wanted him to go away, not her, but she was the one whose heart failed, as though I'd poked the pin through the wrong voodoo doll. I ended up getting rid of both of them. My mother died suddenly. Does anyone ever die gradually? There is no middle ground between breathing and not breathing. She stopped one evening – breathing I mean – and was taken in a slow ambulance far away from me.

The cottage is one of the things from which my new father saved me. His name is Ambrose, and he has excellent posture from his years in the military. When I went to live with him, after the usual suffering and death, this is what I noticed first: when I met him he squeezed my arm, my forearm, with a dry, cool pressure containing welcome and distance, my two favourite things. Ambrose was a quiet man. He's much quieter now, but even in his prime, when I first knew him, he had learned about the power of few words. I never was able to stop rattling on into silences. I wanted to save everyone embarrassment because I didn't know that no one was embarrassed, except for me. Quiet people draw intimacies from me and have an unfair advantage in friendships. Larry is quiet, and when I lie on the sheet beside him he feels to me both warm and cool. I trusted Ambrose because he was quiet and because he never repeated anything I told him.

Ambrose and Peggy came to the funeral home. I was friends with their daughter, Alice, and they wanted me to come live with them, in Alice's old room. Because I was a new orphan. Because they were kind. And I went quietly, secretly in awe of their goodness. Thanks to his Peggy, Ambrose's house was always clean and because they were both Christians nobody around their house drank or smoked or did dope or blew up snakes. Peggy dusted every day, and vacuumed every other. In the early days of my life with them I would come home from school and she would have the carpets folded back on themselves and the furniture askew; the curtains would be off the windows, which smelled of vinegar and newsprint, and the sun bouncing off things would hurt my eyes. She called this spring cleaning, which I had heard of in fiction.

On those occasions I was glad that I had never told anyone about my cottage years. I never was so clean before and as I spent more time in their company, it seemed to me that the years before, with my real family and that man I hated and my molesting uncle and disapproving aunt and delinquent cousins and Bill and Lucia, had happened to someone else, or maybe it was something I'd only read about. If I could stay long enough with Ambrose and get clean enough and buy enough shoes and acquire my Ph.D. then maybe I never was that cottage girl. I look like Ambrose used to look before he went into the sanatorium. Our hair is the same colour and I have his oversized ears and narrow, delicate feet. Our teeth are crooked. For a while I liked to imagine that maybe Ambrose was my real father, full of goodness and kindness. Someone I could never hate.

I didn't hate my real father. He built the kitchen cupboards in our house and included a small hideaway shelf for his bottle of scotch. I heard that he liked Roadrunner cartoons and would hold me on his lap for a few minutes every day after work while he sipped his drink. He died before I was old enough to build a pedestal for him to fall off.

I tried to keep my mother out of the cottage box with all the other memories. I think of her at that kitchen table by herself and not with the other shadows. Whatever the truth was, I think of her as the only person, apart from Ambrose, who enjoyed my company always and thoroughly. I like to manipulate the memories to suit me. I wish Ambrose had some memories to manipulate. I hope that he does and that maybe he's just not saying.

My mother had lime green sheers on the kitchen door and window. It is enough to admit that she loved them. There's no need to go on about the matching lime green no-wax linoleum that she hired the next-door neighbour's unemployed brother-in-law to lay the year that she won the big bingo pot. I wonder what it would be like to go back into that kitchen after my years with Ambrose and his wife. My mother's curtains had white felt polka dots and were ruffled priscillas. I probably couldn't find anything like them now. Probably young retro queens out on their own for the first time are scouring the second-hand shops to find lime green polka dot curtains to put in their kitchens where they will sip mint tea while wearing orange houndstooth polyester bell bottoms. Those curtains are mine. I want them back.

This was all I knew about old people until Ambrose became one. My mother visited Agnes Lacy two afternoons a week, and sometimes I had to go with her though I complained about the raspy sound made by the elastic bandages on her legs when Agnes walked, and about her doily smell of lace and old dust that choked me. I stayed away whenever I could. Agnes was too old.

My mother never lived to be old. Maybe she thought I would spurn her and so got out early. Maybe she wanted to teach me a lesson. Ambrose is getting really old. He never gives me anything any more. Hardly even recognition. But his is a smell on Tuesday and Thursday afternoons that I hold against my face and breathe in deeply, as though he were an expensive sachet.

I know that what I remember is dubious at the best of times. I construct my cottage and my cousins knowing they are all dead or lost to me in other ways; there is no one to confirm or deny. Ambrose won't say what he remembers. He won't say my name but he seems very happy to see me so I believe he recognizes me as someone important to him, but I'm not really, not any more. Not as important as the kind orderly who gets him ready for bed every night because Ambrose won't let the women on the floor touch him. I construct my own significance to maintain my connection with Ambrose whom I love, whether he talks or drools or sleeps. I remember that when I was younger he took me to restaurants and always walked on the road side of the sidewalk. He wore a fedora and took my elbow when we walked, took me up the CN tower and to Niagara Falls and visited or called me every day in the days when he was just beginning to lose his mind, while he could still dial and still converse. To tell me he loved me, making deposits to that account against a future of deficits.

Peggy would phone me in the morning, not wanting to be a bother. "Can you help me get Dad out of bed? Are you busy right now?" and I would hop in the car and scoot down the hill and around the corner, leaving toast to burn. I would run up the stairs to find Ambrose reeking of urine in his undershirt and Jockeys, perched on the edge of the bed. "It's time to wake up, sleeping beauty," I'd say, laughing. "Get ready for true love's kiss." Peggy would take his right hand and elbow and I would take his left and we'd pull. I'd pull against Ambrose's weight, his silent determination, and the laughing I couldn't stop when I looked at him, straining against us, wanting to be left in bed. Why was I laughing? What was so funny? This memory makes me happy. It was almost as if I believed that getting him downstairs would cure him, at least for the day, and I knew I was strong enough to do that. I could deal with that. It was as though I felt reassured that anyone fighting with this much determination would live a long time.

I leave my family at home when I go to the Health Centre. Larry sometimes comes but it's easier for him to stay with the children and he never knows what to say. He doesn't like to see Ambrose the way he is.

Ambrose sits through most of his days now and when he walks he shuffles. His stride is lost. The place he is in is called a Health Centre, which is quite a funny name for it. Sometimes I'm sure that Ambrose finds it as funny as I do. We have the same love of irony. There's a chance he may have Hodgkin's disease, or one of the other more euphemistically termed cancers. The family has decided against a biopsy and the taking of any heroic measures. If they'd asked me I'd have told them I thought

Ambrose was worth any number of heroic measures, even though he's not too clean any more and doesn't make much sense. I tell him he's my dad and I'm his Connie. I tell him I got a new job and I am going to get rich and come get him and the two of us are going to Bermuda. That's when he tells me I am full of beans and I laugh. Words like Bermuda still channel into his consciousness, as though he remembers riding his rented motor scooter along the shore on the one holiday he spent there. He always wanted to go back.

Remembering how to go to the bathroom is hard for him, but remembering Bermuda is easy. Ambrose used to sing, "When I was single my pockets would jingle, I wish I was single again," and a song about Bonnie lying over the ocean, but in his version Bonnie had only one lung, a consequence of a bout with tuberculosis. These songs still make him smile, though he doesn't join in any more.

Sometimes I say to him, "Where are you, Dad? Are you in there?" He doesn't answer me but I like to ask, just in case he really is in there, quieter than ever, annoyed with everyone for talking to him as though he were an immigrant whose grasp of English will improve if we only speak slowly and loudly enough. He eats and sleeps and gets cold, sad, or happy, but I know he's more than the sum of these parts. That's who I talk to and whose hand I hold and whose cheek I kiss. Sometimes he crosses his eyes and blinks like a cartoon of adoration and we laugh together.

The best thing about his old days was curling up beside him on the couch, as though I were small and he were my real father. There is a couch in the Health Centre and if I hold out the KitKat bar at just the right time, he will stop shuffling down the hall and sit beside me while I feed it to him. I can put my head on his shoulder and he might say, How are you, darling, and I might say, Fine.

Larry will dig a symmetrical grave for Ambrose. He will use the backhoe to begin with, after he's carved out the grass and rolled it up like a sleeping bag. Then he'll do the finishing by hand. Ambrose believed he'd be in heaven while we were lowering him in the opposite direction. "Remember, Connie, '*To be absent from the body is to be present with the Lord.'"* I want to know where he is now, when his body is demanding only the merest presence. Does God have the rest?

I imagine that I am devoted to him, that everybody else has shut up once and for all about drinks of juice and what's for supper and why are you going to school when you're so old? I imagine taking my books and papers to balance on my lap in a chair beside him, preparing for tomorrow's seminar, keeping vigil with Ambrose. So that if he should open his eyes and know something, it would be me that he knows. I would like to be known again, to visit that place he made for me.

This is what I want: I want to claim Ambrose's body from the authorities. With my tears, these tears I live with, I would wash his feet and then dry them tenderly with my hair. I want to lay him in a vault, roll a stone in front of it, and mourn him daily. When some days have passed, I want to take some scented oil from the shelf above the bathtub and visit that vault early on a misty, quiet morning. I want to be terrified to see the stone rolled back and light blaze within the tomb. I want two angels wearing lightning to tell me he is risen. I want to be the one with the news.

SHARON STEARNS

Brothers

I saw him born; I was right there. I tried to keep him but it didn't work out. It's probably why I treated him different, years later, and why I have to spit when his name comes up in conversation. I don't mean to say I spit because I hated him; I take after my grandmother in that way – she always spit when she felt too affected by something.

Mum was so big when we came on the boat to Tuk, her stomach sat out in front of her like a throne. My baby sister perched there for most of the trip because Mum was worried she'd toddle off into the sea. I stayed as close to her belly as I could, because I was the oldest boy and she needed me. The sea was big and full of ice that crashed over the side rails and onto the deck. It was noisy too, but I tried not to listen to the ranting, it was too easy to let those dark waves talk me into jumping. That's the thing about me and water, I get this feeling it's where I belong even though I don't know how to swim.

My Dad, Johnny, stayed sober almost the whole way. Probably trying to impress the captain, who was giving him a job on the transport boats and a company house in Tuktoyaktuk. But there was that one night where him and that white trader, Semlin, drank a bottle in the hold. Johnny was all over Mum then, like a greasy old seal. I don't know how she could stand it sometimes, pregnant or not, he was after her, smacking or kissing her depending on his liquored-up state. Sometimes she was laughing with him but lots of times she was hiding too.

Everything Semlin and Johnny did together was a contest. When we lived on Read Island it was always who could trap the most white fox, who could shoot the most caribou, who could drink the most whisky. So when I heard them carrying on that night when the captain said we were only two more days on the water, I knew Johnny was pushing for another win. By the time I got up to watch, he was going pretty good on the guitar and Semlin was singing all these country songs to Mum. I could tell she didn't like it, or maybe she wanted Johnny singing; at least he had a really good voice. Semlin sure liked my Mum, even though he said he hated Eskimo people in general. And he must have done something that night for Johnny to get it into his head that the baby was Semlin's. He must have – why else would Johnny say he'd be damned if he was gonna raise any bastard trader brat? Just wait, he told Mum. If this baby comes out looking too white, it won't spend one day under his roof. The devil can raise it for all he cares.

I saw the look on her face, how she collapsed, like her bones couldn't hold her up and the weight of the baby too. Then her face changed into her *God never gives you more than you can bear* look. It was that picture that froze into my guts and stayed there, like a jag of ice.

So I got the idea I'd take care of it. I was seven – man enough to net fish, feed dogs, and set traps; I could look after a damn baby too.

I'd do anything to wipe that look off my Mum's face.

Not even a month later, barely settled in our new wooden house, that baby decides to come out. I knew it was time because Mum lay down right after supper and asked Johnny to get us kids to bed, then go fetch my Aunt Lucy. I've been waiting for this moment so when I run into the bedroom and say I would take care of the baby if it came out too white, I have a speech prepared that points out all my best qualities. Johnny just laughed but Mum's face crumpled and she told me to shoo off to bed. Using my biggest voice, I turned to Johnny and told him Grandmother Irvana came to me in a dream and if he said no, she was going to put a curse on him so he couldn't hunt or trap or keep his job on the boats and all his family would leave him and go back and live with her on Read Island. My voice came out so strong and clear I thought Grandmother really was putting the words in my mouth. She can do that, even from far away.

Mum struggled out the bed and tried to lead me out of the room before somebody got a slap but she was too late. His big hand flew into my face and the next thing I know I'm socked into Mum's belly and we're wham boom against the wall. As I fall to the floor I'm blinded by a head full of stars so I don't know that I land full on top of her, I only hear her groan then a big swoosh, like all the air coming out of a tire. I'm all wet I think, I must have peed myself and I'm shamed to be seven years old and peed all over my Mum. The stars disappeared and I look down and see Mum holding her shift all soaked. It's her lying in the puddle not me, and I just can't imagine this. I don't have any idea, I'm sure I'm drowning only not in water but in nothingness, in a pool of unknowing.

I'm not big any more; I am small and afraid.

My Dad, all gentle now, picks her up, nearly slipping on the pink water, and lies her on the bed. Suddenly I know it is the baby coming out, it is what made everything so slippery, it is why she is crying. Please don't let it be too white I pray to myself. Please Please let it be a dark brown slanty-eyed boy. My eyes are wide open and I see Johnny's hands cupped between her legs, still and patient. He is murmuring soft words. He is helping her. He is knowing how to take care of her.

I think he has rescued her.

All night I watch and pray for a dark-skinned Eskimo, even though Johnny's taking such good care of Mum I start to wonder if he's changed his mind. If he decides she can't keep it, my plan is to take it to Aunt Lucy's in town. Mum would feel better knowing her oldest boy was keeping an eye on it, that it was staying in the family. I knew some things about babies from my younger brothers and sister, how they could cry for no reason and how rocking them and giving them things to suck on could shut them up. Back then in the fifties, lots of people didn't live in houses or if they did they were mostly canvas or driftwood shacks, but my Aunt Lucy worked as a translator for the government and they put her in one of their white-built houses that had a generator and a gas stove. I liked the idea of living there myself, just to get away from my family, although I'd miss the dogs sometimes. And after a while, I'd take it home for visits and everyone would see it was a well-behaved Eskimo baby. Then I could convince Johnny to bring it back home. For Mum I prayed, all night, until it was born.

I've seen lots of dogs born and it's basically the same thing, except dogs usually have more than one and sometimes twelve or thirteen. They pant, get up, circle nose to bum, then out it plops. Mum panted and moaned most of the night but nothing came out. Not 'til almost morning was it born, so we could have gone to fetch Aunt Lucy after all. Not that it made much difference, Johnny just said it would have been more proper, as getting a baby born was woman's work. A man plants the seed and a woman harvests what's sown, he explained.

Johnny was part Norwegian and Mum's Dad was said to be mostly Scottish, so I was just about to ask him how he was going to decide if the baby was too white when I heard Mum's deep sighing groan, different from the high whining noise she'd been making all night. I snuck up to the bed and sure enough, it was finally coming out. The first thing I noticed were the slanty black slits it had for eyes. Hurray! And when Johnny was wiping it off I saw little testicles and the dark bruise mark staining his tail bone like most of us native-born kids have. He'll be my brother! But then I noticed his skin looked a little creamy now that he was cleaned off.

"Don't get too attached," Johnny said softly to Mum. "My sister Agnes down in Inuvik will know someone who'll take him."

She turned away then, from Johnny, from her newborn son. She wouldn't hold him or put him to her breast, nothing. So Johnny was caught in his own trap; he had to pay attention to the baby, at least until he could find someone else who would. My brother was crying of course, tossing his head back and forth and waving tight little fists in the air, already trying to defend his right to be in the world.

I stood frozen by the bed, trying to will myself to take the baby and run to Aunt Lucy's. But I couldn't move; I was sunk by the picture of Johnny rocking the squalling baby, a look on his face like he was plugging his nose against a terrible smell. And Mum, her dark hair covering her face, sobbing quietly into the mattress. I saw my little sister peaking in the doorway and heard my brothers sniggering behind her. If I had a gun I might have shot us all, just to stop the picture. I had to get out. I couldn't stand to look at anything so hopeless, it was rubbing off on me; I was part of this family after all, our lives, flesh and blood, mingling in the same story.

I ran outside and was surprised to see how bright the sky looked. It was late in the summer and already there had been some frost, but the ground was still brown and the bushes still held leaves, clinging in their stubborn way to the branches. The mosquitoes were almost gone, past their peak. Nothing hates frost more than mosquitoes. You'd think God would have made northern mosquitoes with a layer of fur, but then they are so successful as a plague to man and beast I guess He thought giving them a short season made up for their other advantages.

A thick, fat yellow sun hung just above the horizon, looking huge and old, like the summer was old, and I thought how tired it must be of lighting up the sky for all these endless days. The dark days were coming soon, which would mean rest enough for that old yellow sun. Where it went in winter was a mystery I often tried to unravel; Grandmother Irvana said it slept under a blanket as big as the sky but it was full of holes and when the sun squirmed in its sleep, it shone through the holes and that's what made the northern lights dance. I wasn't sure about this, but thinking about Grandmother and looking at the sun made me feel better, warming the part of me that felt so frozen and helpless.

Other than Aunt Lucy, Grandmother Irvana's sister, we hadn't yet mixed with the people in Tuktoyaktuk. I didn't have an idea of the lay of the land, only that the place seemed very populated compared to the half a dozen families we lived with back on Read Island. Here was a Hudson's Bay store, a community hall, and a small cluster of wooden houses all gathered together in one spot. Spread out around the village were dozens of canvas tents and crummy old shacks.

The National Transportation Company Limited owned most of the boats that freighted cargo all over the Arctic, and the house they gave us to live in was by their boatyard, away from the town, set back on a hill that sloped down to a gravel beach. It was like a dollhouse, with five tiny rooms – an entrance room, a kitchen with an alcove for the table and chairs, and three little bedrooms all in a row in the back of the house.

I ran down the gravel slope to the rocky shore and looked out at the channel that was part of this huge delta that fed water into the Beaufort Sea. A jolly boat was spinning circles offshore. I don't know why we call them jolly boats, they are just ordinary old wooden rowboats; it probably came from the English or Scots people because I can't imagine Eskimos saying a boat was jolly unless it was filled with seals or fish. Even then we would say it was the people who were jolly, and not the boat. Three boys were sitting in the boat. Only they weren't really sitting, at least not the way I sat in a boat; the two on either end were jumping up and down while the middle boy was oaring them around in circles like a madman. It looked like the two jumpers were trying to catch each other off balance so they would fall out of the boat. They were screaming and laughing so they didn't notice me until the boy who was rowing looked to shore. He stopped and yelled, pointing his finger in my direction. All the commotion died in a second; I felt like I was a caribou or bear they had spotted and now they were the hunters. The middle boy pulled his oars toward shore, using long, powerful strokes, as strong as a grown man. When they got close I could see he was the oldest, and when the boat bottom scraped the gravel he ordered the other two to jump out and lead it onto the beach.

Meanwhile, he sat in the boat like he was the big chief, and I guess he was, because they happily jumped out into the ankle-deep water to do his bidding.

Why was there nothing in the boat? No fish, no nets, not even a bailing tin. What were three boys doing out in the channel so early in the morning?

Surrounded before I knew it, these laughing boys closed in, black hair curtaining their eyes, slashes of brilliant white teeth a grinning contrast against their dark skin. Checking me out – friend or enemy, strong or weak? They pushed me around, taunting, jeering, circling, poking me with smooth brown fingers. Worst of all, they were talking in English. I could tell from the rhythm. I knew some words, but it was a mystery, a language I was afraid of. It was powerful. Magic. I didn't understand so I couldn't conjure. Magic is power you don't understand. Like my grandmother – white people were afraid of her because they didn't understand her magic. But I was afraid of the white people and their busy, ruthless words. And I was ashamed that I didn't understand these taunting boys; they'd discovered a weakness right at the start.

I yelled Jesus Christ! Merde! By Christ! Motherfucker! Sacré bleu! – All words I'd heard Johnny use to good effect sometimes. The big one started laughing so hard he fell down and rolled around on the gravel. The other two jumped on top of him to make one big ball of rolling, hysterical boys.

I yelled Son of a bitch! Please! Asshole! Bastard dog! Thank you! Goddamn it! Get lost! It was my big voice, my grandmother voice throwing out sound like a harpoon, but they don't back off, in fact they get up and start running towards me. I back up, hoping to outrun them to my house, knowing it's too far, certain they'll catch me, drag me into the water, probably drown me.

In Eskimo culture the test is always to see how strong you are. If you suffer a lot and are stronger for it, then you are number one in our books. We don't give our dogs too much to eat or drink because a little suffering goes a long way to helping them survive. Too much food would make them soft, and poor prospects for survival when times got tough, as they usually do in the Arctic. Same thing with humans. Some people in the south think we have cruel natures but I say let them try and thrive in the barren lands in forty below. Where you have to kill animals for food, clothing, and shelter. Where it's kill or be killed. When your world is made up of ice and snow and blizzards in the winter and mosquitoes, storms, and blizzards in the summer, you have to be crafty and tough, learn to laugh at hardship, and take pride in the fact that you are alive for another day. Because often it works out that you are alive at the expense of another's death, which makes you the survivor, the strongest one.

So I was prepared to fight to the death when I felt them grab me from behind. When they threw me on the ground I kicked my legs up and managed to connect with Big Chief's chin, knocking him backwards. The other two jumped on my belly and I felt all the air explode out of me. Big Chief got up and gave me a funny look, like he was suddenly dealing with an animal he didn't know. I was trying to get my air back when they dragged me down to the water by my feet. Little bits of gravel slid up my shirt, cutting into my skin. When we got to the water, Big Chief leaned over, grabbed my head, and lifted me up to his face. He was browner than me, and his eyes were wide apart on his face, which made it seem like there was too much space for his nose, or maybe his nose was just very small. His white teeth were dished in, and his hair was black and slippery, like raven feathers.

My name is Henry Nasogaluak, he said, and these are my brothers Joe and David. We came in our boat to see you. We heard about your family moving in here. Then he shoved my head under the water and held it there while I panicked and thrashed, until my fear rose into my throat, higher and higher, until I had no choice but to swallow it. So giving up was a kind of relief, which he must have sensed because that's when he lifted my head and let me breathe again, great sucking gulps filling my lungs.

In our native tongue I gasped out – My name is Peter. It's Peter Norberg and I was born on Read Island and my Mum just had a baby and my Dad is Johnny Norberg and he could kill you if he wanted to.

Henry let me go and his brothers stood back while I crawled onto the beach. They stood with their feet in the water, glistening like seals, smiling, eyes cheering me on, waiting to see what I'd do next.

My Dad said the baby is too white so we're going to give it away, I yelled. You can have it! You want the baby?

Like an offering, like it was something they wanted. They mumbled among themselves and Joe, who looked the youngest, said he thought his Grandma might want a baby if it was a boy and then David piped in saying their Aunt in Paulatuk probably wouldn't mind. Babbling away, all talking at once, they came up with aunts, cousins, nieces, even their own mother who they boasted made the best caribou stew and still had milk in her breasts leftover from their youngest brother. And everything was suddenly ordinary, sorted out and calm; the sun felt high and warm in the sky, warm enough to lure out the last of the mosquitoes, probably drawn by our smell now that we were all friends.

They said, Get in the boat and we'll go ask around. I remembered the sloppy, careless way they handled their boat and knew I couldn't go with them. So to hide my fear of their reckless disregard for the sea, I said I had my own boat, bigger and better and they could damn well drown in theirs, see if I cared. They just laughed and Henry said, If you're so scared to come in our boat, go get the baby. We promise we won't get too crazy with a baby on board.

He's too smart for me, I thought, my face hot with shame. I can only stare at him, caught, as he stares back, his eyes pushing me back up the hill. Tell your dad it's O.K., Henry whispered. We know everybody here. He can be our brother.

O.K! I shouted, shame gone, forgetting to be afraid. Henry grinned and smacked me on the chin – oh we were thick as thieves now, thicker than my own blood. I charged up the hill and into the house.

In the kitchen, Johnny held my brother, all swaddled now and still crying. The other kids hung around the table watching Johnny get a bottle ready. My little sister was sucking on a piece of dry meat, but I could see she was more interested in the bottle. Everyone was avoiding the bedroom.

We're taking the baby, I said to my Dad, stretching out my arms.

Who's we, he snapped. Taking him where?

My friends. They're waiting in the boat. It doesn't matter that he's too white. They know lots of people. They know everybody.

Johnny went to the window and looked out. When he turned back to me his face was closed. Go in and sit with your mother, was all he said.

He's my brother, I screamed, drowning out the baby. Johnny ignored me. He was trying to get the baby to suck on a bottle of Klim, the powdered milk the Hudson's Bay sold. Backward milk I called it, later, when I learned English spelling. I never did learn to drink it. The baby was not impressed either, I could tell by his spastic wiggles and angry cries. All that work to get born, I thought, and the reward is not a soft mother's body with her warm, rich milk, but this hard man with his cold rubber nipple and old, dead milk.

I watched Johnny struggle with his son, his mouth a straight, determined line, his eyes refusing to look at me, to acknowledge me at all. Only the baby in his arms; it was all he could do, all he could see. Stick the rubber nipple into the baby's mouth 'til he choked and sputtered. Take it out. Wait a minute and let baby scream. Stick it in again, more choking, sputtering, screaming, resting.

My brother didn't have a chance. After a while the screams would turn to whimpers.

I wasn't going to wait for his first swallow, the giving in. This is the way it is, I tell him silently. Swallow the hard, cold, world and let it feed you. To stay alive. It must be. I turned away and walked outside.

The younger boys were already in the boat; Henry was standing on the shore, holding an oar, squinting up the hill. When he saw I didn't have a baby in my arms, he laughed and jumped in the boat.

Hey! I waved, speeding down the hill, sliding onto the gravel beach. I don't want to go in your stupid boat! I yell. Henry and his brothers pretend they don't hear me; they oar into the choppy sea. Can't even row straight! I scream. Henry turns to look at me. I can see he's grinning. We'll come back some other time! he shouts. Yeah! We'll come back, brother! I hear them hoop and holler, the word brother bubbling through their laughter.

Brother. They would be my brothers.

I think of Mum lying in her bed without her son, knowing I have to go in there and sit with her. It's all right, she'll tell me. Your brother will be taken care of. He will always be part of this family, even if he's somewhere else. She'll have that look on her face, the same look my brother wears now, in the kitchen, feeding in Johnny's arms.

The boat is slowly making its way out into the sea. Pretty soon the waves will swallow it up. I pick up a handful of rocks and throw them in a steady arc at the boys in the boat, the smooth gravel pebbles spattering over them, not hard like an insult, but softer, more like spit.

MARY WALTERS

Show Jumping

June knew that her husband was falling in love with Krista before he did. At first, it was not anything specific about the way he acted or anything he said, but rather an unusual buoyancy in him that was practically contagious.

Krista was Gregory's research assistant. She was both intelligent and young. She'd gone into her master's program directly following a B.Sc., which led June to conclude that she was likely inexperienced in the ways of the world. Sort of like Gregory, when she thought of it. June was not, herself, so innocent.

He called about noon one warm Sunday late in May to ask what June thought of going to the equine centre.

"Just for an hour or so," he said. "They've got a show down there – mostly kids apparently. Nothing professional. I thought it might be fun to have a look."

He'd gone over to the university at nine, saying he didn't think he'd be home until dinnertime. It was so unlike him to propose an outing, especially when it would interrupt his work, that June found the phone call disturbing. She almost said, "No," just to keep him at the university where he belonged.

But when he'd called, she'd been sitting at the coffee table in the kitchen, staring out the window into the garden, a stack of unread manuscripts at her elbow. The day was clear and hot, and she'd been wishing she were at the lake house instead of in the city.

"Good, then," Gregory said. "We'll pick you up in half an hour."

"We?"

"Krista," Gregory said, as though surprised he hadn't mentioned her. "Her sister's jumping in the show."

With uncharacteristic punctuality, Gregory pulled up the driveway exactly thirty minutes later. Krista smiled a greeting at June as she gave up her seat in the front and moved into the back.

Gregory glanced at June as he backed out of the driveway. "Did I tell you Krista's sister's in the show?"

"You did." June turned a little, doing up her seat belt. "Do you ride as well?"

"Yes," Krista said, shifting across the back seat, perhaps so June could see her better. "I don't compete any more, but I do still ride when I can find the time."

June had never been to the equine centre. She'd admired it often on her way to work, a pleasant stretch of green in the middle of the city. The stables were visible from Park Drive, but the competition area was concealed from the freeway by a number of grassy knolls. It would be nice to have a closer look.

It was as they were walking from the parking lot that June first became aware that she felt like the odd one out. Without meaning to, she didn't think, Krista and Gregory had fallen into step with one another and were walking up the hill ahead of her.

She watched the two of them, Gregory's head inclined a little toward Krista's. In the car, they'd been talking about some pellets they'd been analyzing. Gregory's current research concerned the eating patterns of the Northern Saw-Whet Owl.

June had met Krista before, but she'd never really looked at her. Now that she did, she found her rather oddly proportioned. Her legs were quite long in comparison with her torso, and this made her look taller than she was – which was almost the same height as Gregory. She was slender, with dark curly hair, and she wore glasses. There was something attractive about her look – neat, compact, and slightly scholarly, even in the walking shorts and T-shirt she was wearing that afternoon.

She walked up the hill briskly, and Gregory strode along beside her. He was overdressed in his long-sleeved white shirt, his grey trousers, his grey socks. Sandals were the only concession he'd made to the approach of summer.

Gregory was June's second husband. She'd been married to him five years now, and in that time his dark brown hair and beard, still thick and full, had greyed considerably, and the lines on his face had deepened. In certain men, the passage of time seemed of itself to produce an appearance of substance and validity, and Gregory was one of those.

His expression was often one of intense curiosity, as though the answer to a question he'd been mulling over all his life was now within his grasp – would be provided, in fact, by the very person with whom he was now speaking. Knowing, as June did, that he was often not even listening to the other person made this expression somewhat less appealing, but there was no doubt at the moment that he was listening to Krista.

June reached the top of the hill. Below her, there were two large rings surrounded by white railings. In one, a rider was jumping her horse over low green fences. At a distance, between where June stood and the stables, was a high structure where the announcers and the judges sat. Beyond them, a row of white flags waved in the warm breeze.

By the time June reached Gregory and Krista, they were settled near the area where riders and horses awaited their turns on the course. Gregory had pulled out his pipe and was filling it as June sat down beside Krista.

"Krista started to ride when she was five," he said, tamping the tobacco. "Her sister was even younger."

"Remarkable," June said. She nodded at the course. "How old are these riders?"

"Fourteen, fifteen or so," Krista said. "Deirdre's seventeen. She's on a little later."

"Deirdre is Krista's sister," Gregory said.

June watched one rider after another essay the course, some more successfully than others. Gregory asked a question now and then about the competition, but most of the time he and

Krista talked about undigested fur and insect exoskeletons. Gregory grew enthusiastic as they talked, and Krista seemed as interested as he was.

June was surprised at his energy in the heat until she recognized the symptoms. It was like she wasn't there. A woman nearby looked over at Krista and Gregory, curious at their conversation, and then looked at June beside them.

June, who'd been thinking about Alan and the others, smiled at her – then nodded. She wasn't sure why she'd nodded, but it seemed to confuse the woman, and she looked away.

Gregory had gone to find them something cold to drink but he had been held up, and he started back around the course just as Deirdre was announced to start her ride. He turned to watch, three plastic cups gathered in his hands.

June felt Krista tense as Deirdre started out, pull back as she approached each fence, and then relax as the horse and rider cleared it. Deirdre had been over earlier to talk to them, and June had noticed that she was built like Krista – short torso, relatively long legs – although they didn't otherwise look much alike. Because of her build, Deirdre looked younger in the saddle than she did up close.

She completed four jumps smoothly, and seemed to be riding faster than the others in her class. But at the fifth jump her horse balked, and before June even realized what was happening, Deirdre was thrown forward over the fence to the ground, the horse was heading back toward the starting gate, and Krista was on her feet and running down the hill.

At the railing, Krista stopped. The trainer was out already, running toward Deirdre. She'd grabbed the reins of the horse on her way by and the beast trotted along behind her, docile. Deirdre stirred slowly and sat up, keeping her head down. At the trainer's insistence, she finally stood and took the reins, holding one elbow with her hand. To warm applause, she walked her horse back toward the starting gate.

June was watching Gregory. Drinks clutched in his hands, his eyes, bemused and distant, were on Krista as she moved up the hill toward June. He seemed unaware of Deirdre's accident. In his head, June thought, he and Krista were somewhere miles away.

June saw that Krista was falling in love with Gregory at a reception for a colleague of Gregory's who was leaving for a year of research in Australia. The gathering was ostensibly to wish the colleague well – which no one, in fact, did.

June was there in her capacity as director of the university press. The Australia-bound professor, a parasitologist, had a contract with them to do a book. Gregory was there as a senior member of his department. It was at a similar gathering that June and Gregory had met.

June was a little surprised when Krista appeared. Master's students didn't normally attend these kinds of things. Gregory, who was standing beside June, lost in thought, didn't seem to notice her arrival.

A few minutes later, Krista appeared at June's side, holding a glass of wine. She was wearing a dark red dress, quite short but smart and obviously expensive.

"You wear clothes like that, and you'll have no future in academics," June said.

Krista looked down at her dress, then up at June, concerned.

June smiled. "It was meant to be a compliment. 'Stodgy' is the look we strive for here."

Krista relaxed and smiled. She glanced at Gregory, her expression open, soft. His look was guarded, but there was no missing the attraction.

"How's your sister?" June asked.

Krista paused as though mulling over the question. Then she said, "Bruised elbow. Nothing serious."

"I'm glad to hear it. Dangerous activity, jumping."

Krista nodded solemnly. "They're trying to make protective equipment mandatory. Helmets, anyway. But riders would rather be fashionable than safe."

Gregory had come to life. "They had the same problem with cyclists once," he said, "and now just look at them. I'm sure it will be the same for horseback riders." He paused and, with a smile at Krista, added, "A helmet wouldn't have helped your sister much."

It wasn't the kind of thing that Gregory would normally have said. People didn't spend enough time studying their own behaviour, June decided. They should. They never knew when they'd need to imitate it.

She, single in those days and feeling mighty in her singleness, had been as concerned as Alan – more, it sometimes seemed – that they not get caught, that neither of them by glance or gesture compromise themselves or one another. She didn't want his marriage to disintegrate. She didn't want any part in causing something like that to happen, and she didn't want to deal with the fallout if it did. The affair had lasted nearly a year, and they had continued to work together when it was over. As far as she knew, no one in the office had suspected. As far as she knew, he was still married to the woman they had betrayed.

At the time she hadn't thought much about Alan's wife. She had met her only once, and Alan never talked about her. Since the Sunday at the equine centre, she'd been thinking about her a lot.

"People should be allowed to decide for themselves," she said. "Hockey, horseback riding, cycling. If they want to smash their brains to bits, it should be up to them."

Krista looked away. Gregory nodded, then glanced uncomfortably at Krista.

June said to Krista, "I gather you managed to avoid getting injured? When you were competing?"

Gregory looked down at Krista's leg just an instant before she held out her left foot. She said, "I broke my ankle once. That's when I quit." She smiled and raised her eyes to June's. "I'm afraid I lost my courage."

June looked from Krista to Gregory.

"Surely not all of it," she said.

June said in car on the way home, "I didn't expect Krista to be there."

Gregory shrugged. "She's been working pretty hard. I thought she might enjoy it."

"Why should she? No one else did."

He smiled, not looking at her. "There isn't much going on this time of year. I wanted her to meet a few people in the department."

June was feeling steely. Wine did that to her, gave her an exoskeleton of her own, but there was more to it than that. The way she was able to see through them, Krista and Gregory, made her feel scornful and superior.

As they passed the equine centre she said, mainly to see how he'd respond, "Maybe we should invite her to the lake."

"To the lake."

"For dinner." She looked over at him. "With her boyfriend, if she has one."

His brow had furrowed. "Why would we do that?"

"She's a nice young woman. I quite like her." She looked down at her hands. "Why not?"

Gregory said, "I don't think she has a boyfriend."

"Oh," June said, "she must. An attractive young woman like that? Maybe she just hasn't told you."

"I don't think she does," he said quite seriously.

"Well, then. We could invite the kids." Meaning his, and hers. "They're about the same age she is."

"Oh, no," he said. "I don't think so. They're not at all interested in my work." He shifted in his seat. "The Dicksons might be better."

The wine was wearing off, and June was beginning to have misgivings. She'd been certain he'd refuse, but instead he was warming to the idea. He said as he turned into their driveway, "I suppose I could show her where the owls roost."

June could not stop thinking about those other wives: Alan's had not been the only one. Now that she was becoming one of them, she thought about them all the time.

She had not considered herself a threat to them. She didn't want their husbands, nor did the husbands want to leave their wives. She'd thought of the affairs as good things, small avalanches of intensity and passion in busy, routine lives. Finished in their time – and with no hard feelings afterward on either side. She had always been careful, fastidiously circumspect. She'd believed they'd left no victims.

But perhaps they had. It had never occurred to her that the wives of these men might have known what was going on from the way their husbands had changed. That no matter what she said or didn't say, what she did or didn't do, these women would find out.

How could they not have known? she wondered now. Decent men, their husbands, men like Gregory. They didn't do that kind of thing. And what had the women said, when they recognized what was happening? How had they behaved? In what domestic dramas had she, unknown to her, been given a starring role?

She glanced over at Gregory. They were on their way to the lake, and the trunk of the car was filled with groceries, beer and wine. There would be eight for dinner. The Halburns were coming, and the Dicksons. Jed Dickson's mother, who was staying at the lake, would make the number even. Krista, it turned out, did not have a boyfriend.

June was driving, Gregory reading *Equinox* in the passenger seat, one knee against the door. He was wearing lake clothes – navy shorts, a grey T-shirt – and the light on the dark hairs above his knee, the shape of the knee itself, made her want to weep.

"Do you think there's something missing from our marriage?" she asked him, keeping her voice steady.

He put his finger on the word he'd last read and looked over at her. "Missing? How?"

"A spark or something. I don't know."

"A spark or something," he repeated. He was still looking at her, genuinely puzzled from the sound of it. She'd noticed that he was getting better at dissembling.

"I don't know," she said.

"Is everything all right?"

"Of course. I was just thinking."

Their relationship had been remarkable in her life because of its lack of turmoil. They had met and courted and finally married on such a low key that it had all seemed as natural as going to sleep. It had been almost too peaceful, she'd sometimes thought. It had been dull and unimaginative. It had occasionally been boring.

Other men, including her first husband, had aroused more passion in her, had been able to take away her appetite, and make her temper ragged. But those more emotional relationships had never been coloured by the kind of despair and fear that marbled her feelings now. It did not seem to June that she had ever really been in love before.

As they pulled through the trees beside the lake Gregory stirred himself, yawned and said, "We should get someone out to look at the roof."

He is planning for the future, June thought, and felt her spirits rise.

He's acting like he's planning for the future, she thought, and felt them sink again.

She looked over at him and remembered that she knew him. He's thinking about the roof, she thought. That's all that he is doing.

He was looking at her evenly. Her throat had tightened and she took a breath to loosen it before she said, "That's a good idea."

Krista called at 5:30. She had managed to get lost.

June heard the tenor of Gregory's voice change when he realized who it was. He became bright and attentive, cheerful, as he gave her the directions.

June wondered how she'd make it through dinner when even the sight of the mushrooms she was slicing made her nauseous.

The guests, however, were animated, the evening warm with few mosquitoes. They had their drinks out on the deck, high above the lake, and it was clear from the start it would be a successful party.

Krista looked beautiful. She wore an ivory suit of a loosely woven linen, and she had divested herself of the glasses. She seemed to have acquired an even tan in the weeks since June had seen her last. She was charming and witty, bringing out the best in the other guests – especially the men.

It turned out she was a little older and more experienced than June had thought. She'd travelled for two years following the third year of her baccalaureate program, working on a farm in New Zealand and at a restaurant in Greece. Her travelling companion had stayed behind in England when she'd decided to come home.

"We had nothing in common, really," she said lightly. "He was older than I was. Ready to settle down."

June was doing her best not to drink too much, in order to remember how she normally behaved. She passed out small plates of shrimps and raw vegetables, grateful for the domestic industry that she could carry out by rote.

Just as June was about to ask them to come in for dinner, Krista asked directions to the bathroom. Gregory said he wanted to get Jed an article he'd been reading, and he'd show her where it was. The two of them went into the house.

After several minutes, June went back into the kitchen. She checked through the window that the other guests were occupied, then picked up two clean wineglasses and moved into the doorway to the hall. There she stood still, and listened.

"It's a beautiful place," Krista said, quietly but distinctly.

"I'll show you the boat house after dinner," Gregory said. "There's a family of loons down there."

"That would be wonderful," Krista said in the same measured tone. It was a tone that June knew well, one that said everything but gave nothing away. At least that's what she'd thought at one time.

There was a silence before the bathroom door clicked closed.

June put the glasses on the table in the dining room, then went back to the kitchen and turned on the tap.

Gregory came in and put one hand around her waist. "Great party," he said. "Thanks." He was holding the magazine he wanted to give to Jed, totally unconcerned.

"I shouldn't have invited her," she said suddenly.

"Who?"

"Krista."

"Oh, I think she's having a good time," he said. "She seems to be fitting in quite well."

Smooth, she thought. You're getting very good at this.

"She has a crush on you," she said softly, and felt him flinch.

She turned, but he'd pulled himself together. "Don't be silly," he said. "A girl her age?"

He gave her a brief hug and went outside.

During dinner, Krista and Gregory avoided eye contact. As she put down plates and cleared them, June considered the life that she and Gregory had created with one another, this lake house, these good friends, and wondered how he could risk throwing it away.

But later, in the darkness of the kitchen, she thought that maybe he wasn't risking anything at all – no more than Alan and the others had risked their lives to be with her.

An image of Alan's wife rose up before her, a woman so petite that June had been able to dismiss her from her thoughts for many years.

Maybe it was only the way you saw it – whose eyes you saw it through. Maybe it was up to her this time.

When she came back to the dining room, Jed's mother asked her how she'd made the pie crust, startling her back into the here and now. There was nothing she could do at the moment anyway, except to carry on. She smiled at Jed's mother, and said she'd used a packaged mix.

Later, Gregory would take Krista down to the boat house, and he would show her where the loons were, and the tree where an owl liked to roost. At some point June would go outside and stand on the deck in the darkness for a moment, and she would imagine them together – concealed by trees below her, their words muffled, silenced, by moving leaves and the lap of water. By the time they came back up, she would be inside again, occupied with conversation, pouring coffee, clearing away the dishes.

In the same way, she would wait for Gregory – for as long as she needed to, saying nothing before or after.

She would not be alone. She felt them gathering behind her – Alan's wife, and the others. Malevolent? Perhaps. Vindicated, certainly. Still, she found a peculiar and unexpected strength in knowing they were there.

ALISSA YORK

The Back of the Bear's Mouth

God knows how long Carson was watching me before I caught on – it was dark where he was sitting, like he'd brought some of the night in with him. I matched his look for a second, and a second was all it took. He stood up out of his corner and made for the bar.

I saw this show on the North one time. About the only part I remember was these bighorn sheep all meeting up at the salt-lick. They were so peaceful, side by side with their heads bent low, and no rutting or fighting, no matter if they were old or up-and-coming, no matter if they were male or female, injured or strong. That's the way it was with me and Carson. Neither one of us said much. We just sat there, side by side, and it felt like the natural thing.

When the time came, Carson just stood and made for the doorway, the same slow bee-line stride he'd taken to the bar. Beside me, the bartender cleared our glasses and talked low into his beard, "Think twice little girl, the Northern bushman's a different breed."

But then Carson looked back at me over his shoulder, and just like a rockslide, I felt myself slip off the barstool and follow.

The truck took its time warming up, so we sat together in the dark, both of us staring at the windshield like we were waiting for some movie to start.

"Robin," he said finally, "I figure you got no place to go."

I turned my head his way a little. I was just eighteen and he must've been forty, but none of that mattered a damn.

"No, Carson, I don't."

"Well." He handed me a cigarette and put one to his own lips, leaving it hanging there, not lighted. I brought the lighter out of my coat pocket and held the flame up in front of his face, the flicker of it making him seem younger somehow, a little scared. After a minute I sat back and lit my own.

I must've fallen asleep on the drive. It was no wonder with the kind of hours I'd been keeping – hitching clear across the country in just under three weeks. God knows how I landed in Whitehorse, except I remember hearing some old guy in a truck-stop talking about it, calling it the stop before the end of the line.

I opened my eyes just as Carson was laying me out on the bed. The place was dark and cold as a meat locker. It stunk of tobacco and bacon, oiled metal and mould and mouse shit, but some-where underneath all that was Carson's smell, a gentle, low-lying musk. I know it sounds crazy, but I'll bet that smell was half the reason I went with him in the first place.

I pulled the blanket around me and sat up, watching the shadow that was him pile wood into the stove. He lit the fire, then settled back into the armchair, watching me where I sat. I'd always hated people staring at me. I guess that's why I left school in the end – the teachers and everyone staring at your clothes, your hair, staring into your skull. But Carson was different. His eyes just rested on me, not hunting or digging, just looking because I was there, and more interesting than the rug or the table leg.

Who knows how long we sat like that. I remember him pulling a couple more blankets down from a cupboard, laying one around my shoulders and leaving the other at the foot of the bed.

In the morning, sun was all through the place. The bed was an old wrought-iron double, with only my side slept in. Coals burnt low in the stove. A grizzly head hung over the bed, mounted with its mouth wide open and the teeth drawn back like a trap.

Carson was nowhere, so I stepped outside and lit a smoke. It was warm, the sun already burning holes in the last patches of snow. We were in the bush all right, the clearing was just big enough for the cabin, the outhouse, and the truck. The dirt road that led in to the place closed up dark in the distance, like looking down somebody's throat. A skinny tomcat squeezed out the door of the outhouse and sat washing what was left of one of its ears. The trees grew thick and dark and the sound of jays and ravens came falling.

I found Carson round back of the cabin, bent over the carcass of a deer. There was another one in the dust nearby, a buck with small, velvety antlers. Carson looked up at the sound of my footsteps, his eyes all quick and violent.

"Morning," I said.

"Morning."

"You get those this morning?"

"– No."

Something told me to shut up. I walked back round to the door and went inside. The place looked like it hadn't ever been cleaned, so I threw a log in the stove, put the kettle on top, and set about finding some rags and soap.

He never touched me for the whole first week. A couple of times he walked up close behind me and stood there, smelling my hair or something, and I waited for his hand on me, but it didn't come.

The days passed easily. I got the place clean, beat the rugs and blankets, swept out the mouse shit, oiled the table, and washed the two windows with hot water and vinegar. I even stood up on the bed and brushed the dust out of the grizzly's fur. There were gold hairs all through the brown, lit up and dancing where the sunlight lay on its neck.

Carson never thanked me for cleaning up, and I never thanked him for letting me stay. On my eighth night there he turned in the bed and I felt him pressing long and hard into the back of my thigh. He held me tight, but it didn't hurt. He fit into me like something I'd been missing, like something finally come home.

Carson was sometimes gone for part of the night, or all of it. He either went out empty and brought a carcass back, or went out with a carcass or two and came back empty. Usually it was caribou or deer, but one time there was a lynx. He let me touch the fur. It felt just the same as a regular cat – a few hairs came away in my hand.

Time went by like this, me cooking and cleaning and watching, sometimes reading the *Reader's Digest* or some other magazine from a box in the cupboard, sometimes just sitting and smoking on the doorstep, watching the forest fill up with spring. Carson got more comfortable when I'd been there for a while, started teaching me how to shoot the rifle – first at empty bean tins, then at crows and rabbits that came into the clearing. When I finally hit a rabbit, Carson let out a whoop and ran to get it. Then he took the gun from my hands and held the rabbit up in front of my face. Its hindlegs were blown clear off. I felt my fingers go shaky when I reached for its ears, felt tears come up the back of my throat when I took it from him, the soft, dead weight of it in my hand.

One night I got Carson to let me go along. That sounds like I had to talk him into it, but really all I said was,

"Can I come?"

"You can't talk if you do."

"You heard me talk much?"

"– All right."

It was like driving through black paint – the headlights cut a path in front of the truck, and the dark closed up behind us. I had to wonder how Carson found his way around, how he ever managed to get back home. When we got a ways off the main road, he slowed right down and started zigzagging, the headlights swishing over the road and into the bush, then back over the road to the other side.

I was just nodding off when Carson cut the engine, grabbed the gun, and jumped out into the dark. I caught a yellow flash of eyes in the bush, then came the shots, the gun blazing once, twice, and the moose staggered into the lights, forelegs buckling, head slamming into the dirt. Carson pulled a winch out from under the seat and rigged it up to some bolts in the bed of the truck. We got the moose trussed up, but it took us forever to get it in the back.

"This is a big one," I said, not sure if it was true. I'd only ever seen one from far away, standing stock-still in a muskeg, the way they do.

"Not one," he said, "two. Springtime, Robin."

The next night Carson headed off on his own and I was just as glad. I was still trying to lose the picture of that moose's head hitting the ground.

It seems like it would be creepy being out there in the middle of God-knows-where, Yukon Territory, but I got used to it pretty fast. Even when I was alone it felt safer than any city I'd been through – all those junkies and college kids and cars.

One night, though, I woke up slow and foggy, feeling like I couldn't breathe. It took a while for me to realize the tomcat was sitting on me, right on my chest, and when my eyes got used to the dark I could make out the shape of a mouse in its jaws.

I'm no chicken, but that dead mouse in my face scared the shit out of me. I threw the cat clear across the room and the mouse flew out of its mouth and landed somewhere near the foot of the bed. The tom yowled for a minute, then found the mouse and settled down. I swear I didn't close my eyes until dawn. I just lay there, listening to that cat gnawing and tearing at the mouse, snapping the bones in its teeth.

I'd been out there for about three months as close as I could guess, and I had no ideas about leaving. It wasn't that Carson was such great company – half the time he wasn't there, and the other half he was busy skinning something, or cleaning his guns, or doing God knows what round back of the cabin. At night was mostly when we met up. He'd climb into the bed after me, and hold me hard and gentle, always the same way, from the back with me lying on my side. I didn't mind – it felt good, and I figured he was shy about doing it face to face. It made sense, a man who lives out in the bush on his own for so long.

By that time I was sure I was pregnant. I hadn't bled since I'd been there, my breasts were sore, and my belly had a warm, hard rise in it. One night when Carson was lying behind me, I took his hand and put it there. I turned my face around to him, and even though it was dark as the Devil, I could tell he was smiling. I don't know that I've felt that good before or since.

I only asked Carson about the hunting once.

"Carson, all these animals . . ."

The way he looked at me made me think of that first day, when he looked up from that deer like he was a dog and I was some other dog trying to nose in on the kill. His eyes were really pale blue, sometimes almost clear. They didn't usually bug me, but times like that I always thought of that riddle – the man gets stabbed with an icicle, and it melts, and then where's the murder weapon?

It was maybe a week or two later when I woke up to the sound of Carson coming home in the truck. That alone told me there was something wrong – he usually coasted up to the cabin and came in without waking me up. I was lighting the lamp when he threw open the door.

"Can you drive?"

"What's wrong?"

"Can you drive!"

"Yes!"

"Get dressed."

"What's wrong, Carson?"

"Goddammit, Robin!"

I crawled out from under the covers and grabbed for my clothes. He jumped up on the bed and stood where my head had been, reaching one hand deep into the grizzly's mouth. I thought he'd lost it for sure, but a second later he jumped back down and stuck a fistful of money in my face, twenties and fifties, a fat wad of them.

"There's more up there," he said, "if I don't come back you come and get it, just reach past the teeth and push the panel. And watch you don't cut your hand."

He shoved the truck keys into the pocket of my red mac.

"Carson," I said, and my voice came out funny. I was thinking about what he said, about him maybe not coming back.

"Get going. Lay low in Whitehorse. I'll find you."

"But where will you go?"

"Out in the bush. Get going."

He touched my hair for a second, then held the door open and pushed me outside.

I got a room at the Fourth Avenue Residence. I didn't check in until morning, after spending the whole night driving around in the dark, scared shitless. When dawn came and I finally saw the road sign I'd been hoping for, I felt about two steps from crazy.

Whitehorse was waking up when I pulled into town. I bought a bottle of peroxide at the Pharmasave, and a big bag of Doritos, then I found the Fourth Ave. and parked around back.

First thing I did in my room was eat that whole bag of Doritos, fast, like I hadn't had anything for weeks. Then I took the scissors from the kitchen drawer and cut off all my hair. It fell onto the linoleum and curled around my feet, shiny black as a nest of crows. I left the peroxide on until it burned, and when I rinsed it out and looked at myself in the mirror I had to laugh. And then I had to cry.

I slept the whole day and through the night, and the next morning I went down to the front desk and bought a pack of smokes, two Mars Bars, and a paper. I folded the paper under my arm and didn't look at the front page until I was back in my room. I ate the Mars Bars while I read, and my hunger made me remember the baby. Our baby – mine and Carson's.

PITLAMPER GOES TOO FAR

Conservation Officer Harvey Jacobs was shot and badly wounded late last night when he surprised a lone man pitlamping on a back road off the Dempster Highway. The man who fired at Jacobs is believed to be one Ray Carson, who has a cabin in the area. RCMP have issued a warrant for Carson's arrest and ask that anyone with information pertaining to his whereabouts come forward. Jacobs took a single .38 bullet in his right side. He is currently in intensive care . . .

I lay on my back on the bed, until it felt like the baby was screaming for something to eat. I thought about going out, but I ended up calling for pizza.

I was in the corner store when I heard. The old bitch behind the counter leaned across to me and said, "Did you hear? They got that nut case, Carson."

I looked down at the lottery tickets, all neat and shiny under a slab of Plexiglas.

"They had to take the dogs in after him. Got him cornered up in the rocks of a waterfall, but he turned a gun on them. Well, they had to shoot him, the stupid bugger . . ."

She kept on talking, but that was the last I heard. I closed the door on her voice, walked up the road a ways, and sat down in the weeds. I thought about staying there forever, thought about the grass growing up around my shoulders, turning gold and seedy, then black and broken under the snow.

Then I thought about the baby and figured I better get up.

About the Authors

Mike Barnes is the author of *Calm Jazz Sea*, a collection of poems that was shortlisted for the Gerald Lampert Memorial Award. His stories have been published in *The New Quarterly*, *Descant*, *The Fiddlehead*, *Dandelion*, *The Malahat Review*, and *Blood & Aphorisms*. One of his stories is included in *99: Best Canadian Stories*. "In Florida" is part of a collection of stories, *Aquarium*, to be published by The Porcupine's Quill in fall 1999.

Libby Creelman lives with her family in St. John's, Newfoundland. Her stories have appeared in *TickleAce*, *Pottersfield Portfolio*, *The Fiddlehead*, *The Journey Prize Anthology 10*, and *99: Best Canadian Stories*. Her first collection of short stories will be published by The Porcupine's Quill in 2000.

Mike Finigan is a native of Cape Breton, Nova Scotia. He has travelled across Canada and worked as a meat cutter, tire builder, taxi driver, life-insurance salesman, and Frontier College labourer/teacher, among other jobs. He is now a Language Arts/English teacher at St. Paul's Academy in Okotoks, Alberta. His work has been published in *Pottersfield Portfolio* and *The Antigonish Review*, and a story will appear in *Grain* this fall. He is at work on his first novel, *Stonecrusher*, a story for young people.

Jane Eaton Hamilton's books have been shortlisted for the Lowther, VanCity, and B.C. Book prizes. Her work has won the *Yellow Silk* Fiction Award, the *Paragraph* Fiction Award, the *Event* Non-Fiction Award, the *PRISM international* Fiction Award, the Belles Lettres Essay Award, and the Canadian Poetry Chapbook Contest, and has also been cited in the Pushcart Prize and *Best American Short Stories*. "Territory" won the 1998 *This Magazine* Fiction Contest.

Mark Anthony Jarman's work has appeared in *The Georgia Review*, *Northwest Review*, *PRISM international*, *Best Canadian Stories*, *Concrete Forest*, and *The Journey Prize Anthology 9*. He is a graduate of the University of Iowa's Writers' Workshop, and now teaches at the University of Victoria. He is the author of a novel, *Savage King Ya!*, published by Arsenal Press in 1997, and a collection of short fiction, *New Orleans Is Sinking*, published by Oberon Press in 1998. A new collection of stories will be published by House of Anansi in spring 2000.

Barbara Lambert's novel *The Allegra Series* is being published by Beach Holme Publishers in fall 1999. A novella, "A Message for Lazarus," winner of the 1996 *Malahat Review* Novella Prize, will be published by Cormorant Books in spring 2000 in a collection of her shorter fiction, which will also include "Where the Bodies Are Kept." She lives in Vancouver, and is currently working on a novel set in Italy.

Larry Lynch lives in Miramichi, New Brunswick. His fiction has recently appeared in *The Fiddlehead*, *Canadian Forum*, and *Storyteller*. He has completed a collection of short stories, *Inept*, and a novel, *Keith's Bridge*.

Linda Little lives on a small farm on the north shore of Nova Scotia. She has had stories published in *Matrix*, *The Antigonish Review*, *Dandelion*, and several anthologies. "The Still" is excerpted from her first novel. Currently she is working on a new collection of short stories.

Sandra Sabatini is completing her Ph.D. in English Literature at the University of Waterloo, and is at work on a thesis about babies in Canadian literature (she's had five herself). She has published other stories in a linked series, which includes "The One With the News," about an Alzheimer's sufferer in *The Malahat Review* and *PRISM international*. The collected Alzheimer's stories are forthcoming from The Porcupine's Quill, to be followed by a second volume of stories.

Sharon Stearns, a playwright and short-fiction writer, lives in the B.C. interior. Her plays and stories tend to be historically rooted, celebrating characters and events out of Canada's past. One of her plays – *Hunter of Peace*, about the first woman to explore the Rocky Mountains on horseback – was a Jesse Award nominee for Best New Play and Best Original Music. She is currently working on a new play, a murder mystery set in Dog Pound, Alberta, in 1906.

Mary Walters, a freelance writer and editor, lives in Edmonton. In addition to *Prairie Fire*, her stories have appeared in *The Malahat Review*, *Grain*, *Dandelion*, *PRISM international*, *Chatelaine*, and other periodicals, and have been included in several anthologies. Her first novel, *The Woman Upstairs*, won a Writers Guild of Alberta Award for Excellence in Writing. Her second novel, *Bitters*, will be published by NeWest Press in fall 1999. *Cool*, a collection of short stories that includes "Show Jumping," will be published by River Books in late 2000.

Alissa York was born in northern Alberta to Australian immigrant parents. She has lived all over Canada, and now makes her home in Winnipeg. Her work has appeared in various literary journals and in *eye wuz here*, an anthology published by Douglas & McIntyre in 1996. The winner of the 1999 Bronwen Wallace Award, she has recently completed her first collection of fiction, *Any Given Power*, due out from Arbeiter Ring Publishing in fall 1999, and is currently at work on a novel.

About the Contributing Journals

The Antigonish Review, published four times a year by St. Francis Xavier University in Antigonish, Nova Scotia, features poetry, fiction, reviews, and critical articles from all parts of Canada, the U.S., and overseas, using original graphics to enliven the format. Submissions and correspondence: George Sanderson, Editor, *The Antigonish Review*, Box 5000, St. Francis Xavier University, Antigonish, Nova Scotia, B2G 2W5. E-mail: TAR@stfx.ca Web site: www.antigonish.com/review/

The Malahat Review publishes mostly fiction and poetry, and includes a substantial review in each issue. It is open to dramatic works, so long as they lend themselves to the page; it welcomes literary works that defy easy generic categorization. Acting Editor: Marlene Cookshaw. Assistant Editor: Lucy Bashford. Submissions and correspondence: *The Malahat Review*, University of Victoria, P.O. Box 1700 Stn. CSC, Victoria, B.C., V8W 2Y2.

The New Quarterly publishes a lively and eclectic mix of fiction and poetry, as well as views from the inside of the writer's craft. Winner of the gold medal for fiction at the National Magazine Awards for the last two years, and making regular appearances in *The Journey Prize Anthology*, *The New Quarterly* shows off the work of established writers alongside that of newcomers. Good talk, a good read, and all at a good price ($21.40 for four issues)! Submissions and correspondence: *The New Quarterly*, ELPP, PAS 2082, University of Waterloo, Waterloo, Ontario, N2L 3G1. E-mail: mmerikle@watarts.uwaterloo.ca Web site: watarts.uwaterloo.ca/^^mmerikle/newquart.html

Other Voices is an Edmonton literary journal that publishes fiction, poetry, essays, reviews, and artwork by both new and established writers and artists, often focusing on women's writing and women's issues. Established in 1988, it is published twice a year and receives manuscripts from across Canada, the U.S., England, Ireland, Australia, New Zealand, India, and elsewhere. *Other Voices* is run entirely by a volunteer editorial collective. Submissions and correspondence: *Other Voices*, Garneau P.O. Box 52059, 8210-109 St., Edmonton, Alberta, T6G 2T5.

Pottersfield Portfolio is a triannual journal publishing fiction, poetry, essays, and book reviews. Founded in 1979, it accepts submissions from any geographical region and has published the work of Governor General's Award winners along with writers publishing for the first time. The type of work published in *Pottersfield Portfolio* ranges across a broad spectrum from the traditional to the unusual and innovative. Editor: Douglas Arthur Brown. Submissions and correspondence: *Pottersfield Portfolio*, P.O. Box 40, Station A, Sydney, Nova Scotia. Web site: www.chebucto.ns.ca/Culture/WFNS/pottersfield/

Prairie Fire is a quarterly magazine of contemporary Canadian writing that regularly publishes stories, poems, and book reviews by both emerging and established writers. Its editorial mix also occasionally features critical or personal essays and interviews with authors. *Prairie Fire* publishes a fiction issue every summer. Some of the magazine's most popular issues have been double-sized editions on cultural commentaries, individual authors, or specific genres. *Prairie Fire* publishes writing from, and has readers in, all parts of Canada. Editor: Andris Taskans; Fiction Editors: Heidi Harms and Susan Rempel Letkemann. Submissions and correspondence: *Prairie Fire*, Room 423 – 100 Arthur St., Winnipeg, Manitoba, R3B 1H3.

Queen's Quarterly, founded in 1893, is the oldest intellectual journal in Canada. It publishes articles on a variety of subjects and consequently fiction occupies relatively little space. There are one or two stories in each issue. However, because of its lively format and eclectic mix of subject matter, *Queen's Quarterly* attracts readers with widely diverse interests. This exposure is an advantage many of our fiction writers appreciate.

Submissions are welcome from both new and established writers. Fiction Editor: Joan Harcourt. Submissions and correspondence: *Queen's Quarterly*, Queen's University, Kingston, Ontario, K7L 3N6.

Storyteller, "Canada's Short Story Magazine," aims to help bring the popular short story back into the mainstream of Canadian fiction. It publishes a wide variety of styles and genres, with the focus on entertainment. Comedy, mystery, Canadiana, adventure, science fiction, and more combine to produce a different package every issue. This diversity, along with the large number of stories published, makes *Storyteller* unique among Canadian magazines. Submissions and correspondence: *Storyteller*, 43 Lightfoot Place, Kanata, Ontario, K2L 3M3. Web site: www.direct-internet.net/~stories

This Magazine is Canada's best-known alternative magazine of politics and culture. Thirty-three years old, *This* publishes a unique mix of literature, poetry, investigative journalism, and analysis, as well as literary journalism and arts reporting. Devoted to publishing the best new work of emerging and established writers and poets, *This* continues to win both National Magazine Awards (nine in 1997 alone) and other kudos for its intelligence, wit, and innovation. Editor: Sarmishta Subramanian. Submissions and correspondence: *This Magazine*, 401 Richmond St. W. #396, Toronto, Ontario, M5V 3A8. E-mail: thismag@web.net

Submissions were also received from the following journals:

The Capilano Review
(North Vancouver, B.C.)

Event
(New Westminster, B.C.)

Dalhousie Review
(Halifax, N.S.)

Exile
(Toronto, Ont.)

Descant
(Toronto, Ont.)

The Fiddlehead
(Frederiction, N.B.)

Grain
(Regina, Sask.)

Green's Magazine
(Regina, Sask.)

Kairos
(Hamilton, Ont.)

Matrix
(Montreal, Que.)

The New Orphic Review
(Vancouver, B.C.)

On Spec
(Edmonton, Alta.)

Parchment
(North York, Ont.)

*The Prairie Journal of
Canadian Literature*
(Calgary, Alta.)

PRISM international
(Vancouver, B.C.)

sub-TERRAIN Magazine
(Vancouver, B.C.)

TickleAce
(St. John's, Nfld.)

*The Toronto Review of
Contemporary Writing
Abroad*
(Toronto, Ont.)

The Journey Prize Anthology
List of Previous Contributing Authors

* Winners of the $10,000 Journey Prize
** Co-winners of the $10,000 Journey Prize

I
1989

Ven Begamudré, "Word Games"
David Bergen, "Where You're From"
Lois Braun, "The Pumpkin-Eaters"
Constance Buchanan, "Man with Flying Genitals"
Ann Copeland, "Obedience"
Marion Douglas, "Flags"
Frances Itani, "An Evening in the Café"
Diane Keating, "The Crying Out"
Thomas King, "One Good Story, That One"
Holley Rubinsky, "Rapid Transits"*
Jean Rysstad, "Winter Baby"
Kevin Van Tighem, "Whoopers"
M.G. Vassanji, "In the Quiet of a Sunday Afternoon"
Bronwen Wallace, "Chicken 'N' Ribs"
Armin Wiebe, "Mouse Lake"
Budge Wilson, "Waiting"

2
1990

André Alexis, "Despair: Five Stories of Ottawa"
Glen Allen, "The Hua Guofeng Memorial Warehouse"
Marusia Bociurkiw, "Mama, Donya"
Virgil Burnett, "Billfrith the Dreamer"
Margaret Dyment, "Sacred Trust"
Cynthia Flood, "My Father Took a Cake to France"*
Douglas Glover, "Story Carved in Stone"
Terry Griggs, "Man with the Axe"
Rick Hillis, "Limbo River"

Thomas King, "The Dog I Wish I Had, I Would Call It Helen"
K.D. Miller, "Sunrise Till Dark"
Jennifer Mitton, "Let Them Say"
Lawrence O'Toole, "Goin' to Town with Katie Ann"
Kenneth Radu, "A Change of Heart"
Jenifer Sutherland, "Table Talk"
Wayne Tefs, "Red Rock and After"

3
1991

Donald Aker, "The Invitation"
Anton Baer, "Yukon"
Allan Barr, "A Visit from Lloyd"
David Bergen, "The Fall"
Rai Berzins, "Common Sense"
Diana Hartog, "Theories of Grief"
Diane Keating, "The Salem Letters"
Yann Martel, "The Facts Behind the Helsinki Roccamatios"*
Jennifer Mitton, "Polaroid"
Sheldon Oberman, "This Business with Elijah"
Lynn Podgurny, "Till Tomorrow, Maple Leaf Mills"
James Riseborough, "She Is Not His Mother"
Patricia Stone, "Living on the Lake"

4
1992

David Bergen, "The Bottom of the Glass"
Maria A. Billion, "No Miracles Sweet Jesus"
Judith Cowan, "By the Big River"
Steven Heighton, "A Man Away from Home Has No Neighbours"
Steven Heighton, "How Beautiful upon the Mountains"
L. Rex Kay, "Travelling"
Rozena Maart, "No Rosa, No District Six"*
Guy Malet De Carteret, "Rainy Day"
Carmelita McGrath, "Silence"
Michael Mirolla, "A Theory of Discontinuous Existence"
Diane Juttner Perreault, "Bella's Story"
Eden Robinson, "Traplines"

5.
1993

Caroline Adderson, "Oil and Dread"
David Bergen, "La Rue Prevette"
Marina Endicott, "With the Band"
Dayv James-French, "Cervine"
Michael Kenyon, "Durable Tumblers"
K.D. Miller, "A Litany in Time of Plague"
Robert Mullen, "Flotsam"
Gayla Reid, "Sister Doyle's Men"*
Oakland Ross, "Bang-bang"
Robert Sherrin, "Technical Battle for Trial Machine"
Carol Windley, "The Etruscans"

6
1994

Anne Carson, "Water Margins: An Essay on Swimming by
    My Brother"
Richard Cumyn, "The Sound He Made"
Genni Gunn, "Versions"
Melissa Hardy, "Long Man the River"*
Robert Mullen, "Anomie"
Vivian Payne, "Free Falls"
Jim Reil, "Dry"
Robyn Sarah, "Accept My Story"
Joan Skogan, "Landfall"
Dorothy Speak, "Relatives in Florida"
Alison Wearing, "Notes from Under Water"

7
1995

Michelle Alfano, "Opera"
Mary Borsky, "Maps of the Known World"
Gabriella Goliger, "Song of Ascent"
Elizabeth Hay, "Hand Games"
Shaena Lambert, "The Falling Woman"
Elise Levine, "Boy"
Roger Burford Mason, "The Rat-Catcher's Kiss"

Antanas Sileika, "Going Native"
Kathryn Woodward, "Of Marranos and Gilded Angels"*

8
1996
Rick Bowers, "Dental Bytes"
David Elias, "How I Crossed Over"
Elyse Gasco, "Can You Wave Bye Bye, Baby?"*
Danuta Gleed, "Bones"
Elizabeth Hay, "The Friend"
Linda Holeman, "Turning the Worm"
Elaine Littman, "The Winner's Circle"
Murray Logan, "Steam"
Rick Maddocks, "Lessons from the Sputnik Diner"
K.D. Miller, "Egypt Land"
Gregor Robinson, "Monster Gaps"
Alma Subasic, "Dust"

9
1997
Brian Bartlett, "Thomas, Naked"
Dennis Bock, "Olympia"
Kristen den Hartog, "Wave"
Gabriella Goliger, "Maladies of the Inner Ear"**
Terry Griggs, "Momma Had a Baby"
Mark Anthony Jarman, "Righteous Speedboat"
Judith Kalman, "Not for Me a Crown of Thorns"
Andrew Mullins, "The World of Science"
Sasenarine Persaud, "Canada Geese and Apple Chatney"
Anne Simpson, "Dreaming Snow"**
Sarah Withrow, "Ollie"
Terence Young, "The Berlin Wall"

10
1998
John Brooke, "The Finer Points of Apples"*
Ian Colford, "The Reason for the Dream"
Libby Creelman, "Cruelty"

Michael Crummey, "Serendipity"
Stephen Guppy, "Downwind"
Jane Eaton Hamilton, "Graduation"
Elise Levine, "You Are You Because Your Little Dog Loves You"
Jean McNeil, "Bethlehem"
Liz Moore, "Eight-Day Clock"
Edward O'Connor, "The Beatrice of Victoria College"
Tim Rogers, "Scars and Other Presents"
Denise Ryan, "Marginals, Vivisections, and Dreams"
Madeleine Thien, "Simple Recipes"
Cheryl Tibbetts, "Flowers of Africville"